OPERATION DOLPHIN SPIRIT

a Poppy McVie adventure

Titles by Kimberli A. Bindschatel

The Poppy McVie Series
Operation Tropical Affair
Operation Orca Rescue
Operation Grizzly Camp
Operation Turtle Ransom
Operation Arctic Deception
Operation Dolphin Spirit
Operation Wolf Pack

The Fallen Shadows Trilogy
The Path to the Sun (Book One)

OPERATION
DOLPHIN
SPIRIT

KIMBERLI A. BINDSCHATEL

Turning Leaf Books · Traverse City, MI

Published by Turning Leaf Productions, LLC.
Traverse City, Michigan

www.PoppyMcVie.com
www.KimberliBindschatel.com

Print ISBN-13:9780960026104

This is a work of fiction. Names, characters, businesses, places, events and incidents are either the products of the author's imagination or used in a fictitious manner. Any resemblance to actual persons, living or dead, or actual events is purely coincidental.

Thank you for purchasing this book and supporting an indie author.

For Kelly and Nicole—
Thanks for all you do to help further our
understanding of these most intriguing animals.
Your research matters—to them and to us.

And to the brave men and women of the U.S.F.W.S. and
their counterparts around the globe who dedicate their
lives to save animals from harm. Their courage and
commitment is nothing short of inspiring.

May their efforts not be in vain.

For instance, on the planet Earth, man had always assumed that he was more intelligent than dolphins because he had achieved so much—the wheel, New York, wars and so on—whilst all the dolphins had ever done was muck about in the water having a good time. But conversely, the dolphins had always believed that they were far more intelligent than man—for precisely the same reasons.

~ Douglas Adams, *The Hitchhiker's Guide to the Galaxy*

OPERATION
DOLPHIN
SPIRIT

CHAPTER 1

A dolphin lay sprawled on the sand. A gaggle of onlookers had gathered around, snapping pictures and generally looking anxious.

The dolphin's eyes were closed. The poor thing looked dead. It lay still. No movement, no breaths. My stomach clenched. Were we too late? I knew from my experience in Norway that dolphins can hold their breath for a very long time. It could be all right. But I wasn't sure what was happening. I was pretty sure being stranded was not good, and wasn't a common occurrence.

The thing was, I was here in Bimini undercover as a marine mammal research intern, but I knew next to nothing about dolphins. I had a whole book about them in my suitcase. But I couldn't possibly have prepared for this scenario in the time allotted. Hell, I couldn't have prepared for this if I had read all the books I could get my hands on.

I had arrived on the island less than an hour ago expecting to settle in and soak up a little sun before jumping into the mission. No such luck. I slept hard on the flight to Miami but now I was kicking myself for not using the time to do some more research on dolphins. I was not prepared for this. What were the odds it would happen the day I got here?

The extent of my current knowledge of dolphin physiology consisted of what I'd read on Wikipedia on the plane—things like dolphins have teeth and breathe air. But, honestly, I'd thought I could wing it. On a regular day, weren't interns expected to make coffee and file endless stacks of folders? But this wasn't a regular day. A dolphin was stranded on shore, dying. I needed to get up to speed and fast. I willed it to live, racking my brain for anything I could do to help.

I was no nurse, and even if I were, this was no ordinary patient. Water glistened on its back, giving it a sparkly, surreal appearance, a reminder that it didn't belong out of the water, under the sun. It was out of its world. Vulnerable. I felt helpless, wringing my hands, not knowing what to do. I couldn't stand to see an animal suffer.

I gazed up at the noon sky. A day like today had to be the worst. The sun scorched the sand. The air was too thick to breathe. A flock of laughing gulls swooped about, biding time, waiting for an easy meal.

Kerrie Malone, the dolphin researcher I was sent to work with, headed straight for the distressed animal, shooing people away, her two children tagging along after her. They had all come to greet me at the ferry dock and we'd barely had time for introductions when she got the call.

Kerrie approached the dolphin slowly, cautiously, easing to her knees in the sand next to it. As she leaned over the animal, an eye opened and looked up at her.

A flutter of excitement went through me. It was alive.

The dolphin took a breath, drawn and labored, as though it was difficult to do while lying on the sand, gravity bearing down on it. I wanted desperately to comfort it but didn't know how. I knew better than to touch it. I tried to say with my eyes, telepathically communicate, that we meant no harm, that we were here to help.

A commercial float plane revved its engine and taxied out into the bay. It turned into the wind and the pilot put the throttle down. The propellers' roar rumbled across the water as it went, then lifted off, turned, and disappeared behind the trees. I watched it go, wishing it had dropped me off a day earlier.

The dolphin made no sign of fear or being disturbed by the plane. Maybe it had given up or maybe it was injured. "Please, please don't give up," I silently willed it.

Kerrie reached into the dolphin's mouth, took a hold of its tongue, and gave it a gentle yank. The dolphin squirmed, trying to pull away from her. This made Kerrie smile. Must have been a good sign. It still had the will to live. It didn't seem fearful or react violently. Intelligent eyes focused on Kerrie, submitting to her aid. I decided the dolphin knew that she was there to help.

Kerrie stood and heaved a sigh of exhaustion. She looked tired. Not sleepy, but a deep-seated weariness. I didn't know if it was because she knew the long hours of work that lay ahead or if she had carried this fatigue to the beach with her. Either way, she pushed her sweaty blonde bangs off her forehead and went to work, shouting orders at the five men who were there to help while her son, Billy, clung to her leg. The boy must have been about four, blonde and blue-eyed, with a worn-to-threads stuffed turtle clutched in his little hand. Behind him was a younger sister, bouncing to and fro, occassionally trying to stuff fistfulls of sand into her mouth. *Ugh, why do kids put everything in their mouths? Little scavengers...* She must have been fresh out of diapers. Maybe that explained Kerrie's weariness.

The men went to work and Kerrie dropped back down to her knees and began to dig sand from under the dolphin's flipper, allowing for it to hang below the body naturally rather than stay pinned against the ground. Billy dropped the turtle and tried to dig alongside his mother, pushing more sand into the hole than out of it.

"Can I help?" I asked.

Kerrie glanced at me. "Yes, great."

I headed for the other side of the dolphin.

"Take my kids over there," she said, pointing at a cluster of trees, "into the shade, and keep an eye on them. It's too dangerous to be this close."

"Oh. Uh." I looked down at the dolphin, then at her children. "Sure." Watch the kids. Was this typical intern duty?

I tried to take little Charlotte by the hand but she yanked it away. "C'mon," I said, "Let's go over here."

The girl toddled away from me. I followed and tried, once again, to take hold of her hand. She yanked it free with a fearful scowl, then started to cry.

"I'm not going to hurt you." *God, I'm terrible at this.*

How was I supposed to get her to go with me?

"C'mere Girl. Come on!" I slapped my hip. "Who's a good girl? C'mon with me."

Kerrie glanced up at me with an expression that said, have you lost your mind?

Great...

Charlotte took off in an awkward toddle-run toward the water. Billy saw this and giggled while he ran after her.

Shoot! Can kids swim? When did I learn? I don't remember ever not knowing.

I ran after them. "Billy! Charlotte! Stop right this instant!" Amazing how in the presence of children you immediately turn into your mother. I cringed at the thought.

Dealing with kids wasn't exactly my strong suit. Okay. It wasn't my suit at all. Not that I don't like kids. I just never had time with any. Give me a dog. Or any other animal. A dolphin. That I could manage. I'd even been bitch-slapped by a giant sea turtle once and didn't lose my grip. But kids? Yikes.

I scooped squirming Charlotte up just as she took her first steps into the water. "What were you planning on doing? Swimming to Miami? There are jellyfish in there, little girl." I looked around. "I think."

Charlotte arched her back and let out a red-faced, piercing scream. "Hush little baby," I tried to rock her but this was like trying to get a decent grip on an eel. A loud one.

I felt something slam into my legs. "Let go Lotty!" Billy banged his fists on my thighs doing his best to protect his sister from me, the wild-haired monster.

"Hey, hey, it's okay, she's okay," I shifted Charlotte's weight to free a hand so I could reach for Billy, but he dodged me with that crazy ninja quickness tiny people seem to have. This time, when he rammed me, I was off balance trying to keep a grip on Charlotte and we all went over into the surf.

I was trying to simultaneously put Charlotte back on her feet, spit sand and seawater out of my mouth, and wipe my wet hair out of my eyes with my forearm when I heard a familiar laugh. Oh god, not now. *How does he always find me at my most awkward moments?*

"Hey, buddy, want to look through my binoculars?" Dalton squatted near Billy, holding out his prize. Billy gladly took them, grinning.

"Me too! Me too!" Charlotte headed toward her brother, small hands grasping like little crab pinchers while she toddled.

With the kids distracted, Dalton turned to me while I tried to tame my wet curls. "You look good with kids, McVie," he teased, his eyes flashing amusement.

"Oh shut it, Dalton," but I was smiling, relieved he had saved me from coming unglued. "What're you doing here? I thought you were coming in tomorrow?"

"I changed my flight. I thought we might be able to spend some time together on the island before hitting the ground running." We both looked over to the dolphin. "Doesn't look like that's going to work out as planned." Dalton turned back to me. "I headed straight here when I heard about the stranding, but then I saw you being attacked by the most vicious of beasts."

I punched him in the shoulder while he laughed. We walked over to the kids and Charlotte immediately took Dalton's hand when he offered it.

"How are you so good with kids?"

"Oh, I uh," he cleared his throat. "I basically raised my younger brother and sister." He never took his eyes off the kids, clearly uncomfortable with the topic. "Hey, guys! Let's race!" Charlotte and Billy squealed after him, the three of them churning up sand and laughter.

I had thought about Dalton in a lot of different ways, but hadn't considered that he'd make a great father. He was a complete natural. And he had a brother and sister?

A golf cart came to a halt at the edge of the beach and a young Bahamian woman, about my age, trim and athletic with shiny black hair pulled into braids, got out and started to untie the poles and tarp that had been strapped onto the back of the cart. An older woman, gray-haired, round and soft, took a little more time to get out of the passenger side. The kids ran to her squealing, "Maria, Maria." My kid-watching duties were over. *Thank God!*

"Oh good, you're here," Kerrie said, rushing to help untie the load.

Dalton and I exchanged a knowing glance.

"I'll be in the crowd," he said and I followed Kerrie to help.

The young lady nodded at me in the way of a greeting as she yanked on the strap to release it. "You must be Poppy. I'm Natalie."

"Nice to meet you. You're Kerrie's research assistant, right?"

"Give me an update," Kerrie said, impatient.

"I double-checked the tide chart," Natalie said, turning her attention to Kerrie and the problem at hand. "High tide is in six hours. Ralph's making a stretcher."

"Great."

Natalie's attention moved to the dolphin on the beach. "Hey, is that one of the—"

"Yes," Kerrie said, giving her a silencing look. "Let's just focus on getting it back into the water, okay?"

"Sure." She turned to me with an apologetic smile. "It seems you've arrived at a crazy time."

"I take it this isn't very common?"

"No. Not here on Bimini anyway. And I hope it isn't like last time."

"Last time?" This had happened before?

Kerrie motioned for Natalie to keep moving. She grabbed the buckets and towels from the front seat and followed Kerrie to the dolphin.

Two of the Bahamian men who were there to help, with Kerrie's direction, took the poles and tarp and started erecting a shelter over the dolphin—a kind of makeshift pop-up tent—while another dug sand from under the dolphin's other flipper.

Another local man took the towels from Natalie and dunked them in the ocean. Kerrie gave Natalie directions to cover the animal with the wet towels, then continually pour water over it to keep it cool. The man was to keep the buckets coming. He nodded in understanding, concern etched on his face.

I stood there with empty hands. "I can help," I said. "Is there another bucket?"

"You know, if you could keep the crowd back," Kerrie said without looking at me.

I glanced at the small group of onlookers. Everyone seemed to be keeping a respectful distance. In other words, Kerrie was telling me to stay out of the way.

I couldn't blame her. She'd received a phone call not two

days ago from the president of the university with a non-negotiable demand to take me on as an intern. No doubt, she thought I was the spoiled daughter of some rich donor. She'd do her duty and deal with me. But I doubted very much that she liked me being forced upon her. She saw me as someone she'd have to babysit.

It was all right. I *had* been handed the intern job on a silver platter by my Uncle—Uncle Sam, that is. And I'd played the role of the spoiled daughter before. But in this setting, I didn't feel it would serve my purpose. I needed these ladies to like and trust me. "I can keep an eye on the crowd and carry buckets. Please let me help."

Kerrie looked as though I was pressing the last bit of patience she had.

"Okay, you can help Natalie. Whatever she tells you to do. Just…don't touch the dolphin." She turned away from me, shaking her head and reaching for her phone.

"Don't mind her," Natalie said, leaning toward me. "She's in super-stress mode. She feels responsible for all the dolphins here in Bimini."

"I can imagine."

She took the bucket from the man and slowly poured the cool sea water over the dolphin's back, then handed the bucket back to him to be refilled. "She's calling the Bahamas Marine Mammal Stranding Network now. It's the standard protocol. She'll give details and they'll advise her from there."

"But I thought she was a marine biologist."

"She is. But she's not a veterinarian."

Made sense.

Natalie retrieved a carrying case from the golf cart and gave Maria the nod to leave with the kids.

I joined her next to the dolphin. She handed me a clipboard and a measuring tape. "Hold that," she said. I was reminded of my experience in Mexico helping document the sea turtles there.

Kerrie, with the phone held to her ear, knelt in the sand on the other side of the dolphin. "The animal is alert and responsive. Labor in respiration is minimal."

Natalie handed Kerrie a thermometer, stethoscope, and syringe from the case. Kerrie worked quickly, taking the animal's temperature, listening to the heart rate, and getting a blood sample.

"Get the rest," she told Natalie, still on the phone.

Natalie motioned for me to come around to the other side of the dolphin. I took one end of the measuring tape while she took down the numbers. "It's alright. You're going to be alright," she whispered to the dolphin as she moved around it.

She scribbled a few notes, then poured another bucket of water over the dolphin. "They are at high risk out of the water. Exposure to the wind and sun can dry the skin and they can get overheated."

"Hyperthermia," I said.

"Right. Their skin absorbs heat, the blubber retains it, and the circulatory system that normally helps to dissipate heat can't keep up. That's why we need to continually pour the water over it. Especially near the—"

"The flippers, dorsal fin, and fluke—the areas that are thin and highly vascularized," I said, remembering what Dr. Parker had taught me in Norway about the killer whales, which are members of the dolphin family, so I figured I was on pretty stable ground.

"Right," she said with a smile. "But carefully." The man arrived with another bucket of water and she gestured for me to take it. "Lower the bucket as close as possible when you pour. You don't want to startle it. And careful at the blowhole. Pour water there only right after it's taken a breath."

"Gotcha," I said. I could do that. I tipped the bucket and carefully let the water gently cascade onto the towels as I moved from its head to the fluke.

"Make sure no sand gets in the eyes or the blowhole."

"Okay." I could do that, too.

She sighed. "I hate this helpless feeling. The waiting." She crossed her arms, anxious.

I gave the bucket to the man to refill. "Are we waiting for blood results? Seems like—"

"No. That would take too long. We do that for hematologic and plasma chemical analyses, for a long-term prognosis. But right now, we do a quick analysis to determine if the animal is healthy enough to be put back to sea, if we should try to transport it to the rehab facility at Atlantis on the main island, or—" she hesitated "—if we should euthanize it."

"Oh," I said, looking at this beautiful creature, lying here, prone on the beach, not sure I was ready to hear the conclusion. "And?"

"Oh, this one is doing okay. There are no obvious signs of shock or vascular collapse. It's got a good chance."

I let out my breath, relieved. "So, what are we waiting for?"

"The tide. It will help us get it back out to sea." She pointed. "It's too shallow right now."

The dolphin drew in another breath, shuddering with the effort. Natalie's expression matched my feelings. Frustration. The sooner we could get the dolphin back into the water, the better. Waiting for the tide was going to be exasperating.

Regardless, I had a job to do. My directive had been deliberately vague, something like "go see what's happening, if anything, with the dolphins down there." Apparently some high-level government agency had received some intel, but wanted my team—myself and three other agents—to approach the situation with fresh eyes. It wasn't a typical assignment for an elite task force of federal agents. Regardless, we'd boarded the next plane to see what we could find out.

We had suspected something might be going on with the captive "swim with the dolphin" programs. But those were in Nassau, on the main island, over a hundred miles away. Here, there were only boat tours to swim with wild dolphins.

My partner, Special Agent Dalton, had arranged for a job as a divemaster on a local boat. Because he was a Navy SEAL, certification wasn't a problem. My other teammates, Tom and Mike, were posing as a couple of fishermen. We'd expected to ease into the operation, take a few days to get a feel for the situation, the lay of the land. I hadn't anticipated this.

This was as good a time as any, while we waited for the tide, to get more information about the big picture, like how this dolphin ended up here. "You said there was another stranding recently? And it was worse?"

"Yeah," she said with a sigh, "a few years ago. That was a mass stranding event. Now that I see this dolphin, I'm pretty sure it's the only one."

"How do you know that?"

"Well, for one, no bleeding at the ears."

"Omigod, what would cause that?"

Kerrie ended her call. "There are no other strandings reported," she said.

"Good, I'm so glad," Natalie said. "Last time was too sad."

"What happened last time?"

"Two minke whales, a spotted dolphin and fourteen beaked whales were stranded all at once. The Navy was testing sonar equipment not far from here. The sound literally drove the cetaceans out of the sea. They're so sensitive to underwater sound, that—" she paused, "what am I saying? I'm sure you know about that. You're studying marine biology."

"Actually, I'm an ornithology student," I said. I figured it was safer to masquerade as a bird expert, of which I'm quite knowledgeable, who weaseled her way into an internship here, versus a marine mammal expert, which I am not, who should know stuff. My thirty minutes of speed-reading on the plane wasn't going to carry me. Even coupled with what I'd learned in Norway from Dr. Parker. "I mean, I'm really interested, but it's not my main subject. Cetaceans that is. So, assume I know nothing."

Natalie gave me a look of confusion, then turned to Kerrie.

Kerrie managed to hold back an eyeroll. "It's all been approved," she muttered.

"But—"

"Just don't worry about it," she snapped.

By Natalie's reaction, it was clear that Kerrie wasn't usually one to snap at her.

"Oh-kay," she said.

I acted oblivious. "So, you were telling me about the mass stranding."

"Huh? Yeah. The U.S. Navy blasted their sonar not far from here. Fortunately, after five weeks of denial, in a rare historical event, they actually took responsibility, confirming the long held hypothesis that naval maneuvers had been causing most of the recorded stranding events over the years."

"How exactly does the sonar impact the whales?"

"Well, for one, it hurts like hell. We found them with bleeding ears. The necropsies showed cranial lesions and hemorrhaging, suggesting a pressure wave, or intense acoustical energy, had caused the trauma."

"That sounds awful." I winced. "Pardon the pun."

"It was. They were otherwise healthy."

Two men on two separate fishing boats pulled up to shore. Kerrie rushed over to them, pointing at something out in the water.

"What's that about?" I asked Natalie.

"This dolphin will be disoriented and lethargic once we get it back into the water. It's going to take a while, maybe an hour or more, to get it swimming again. They'll patrol for tiger sharks and keep them away."

"Wow. Sharks? I wouldn't have thought of that. So why did this dolphin get stranded? The Navy again?"

She shook her head. "No. We don't think so. There are other reasons that a single dolphin could get stranded. Usually with *Tursiops*, they strand solo only when they're ill, although, sometimes, it's as simple as a juvenile that doesn't know the area, follows some fish into the harbor, and gets caught by the tide."

"Is that what happened here?"

"Most likely, because this particular dolphin probably never—"

Kerrie came up beside her. "We don't want to speculate. Let's get it back in the water first, then we can discuss any evidence we have."

Her response was a typical approach of a scientist—gather evidence first. But something wasn't right. She knew more than she was saying about this dolphin. Both of them did. Kerrie was either involved in whatever I was sent to uncover, or already knew a lot about it. I needed to tread carefully.

While we waited, I dug my hat out of my bag, slathered on some sunscreen, and, with a quick Google search on my phone, learned that this dolphin was a bottlenose dolphin, the genus *Tursiops*, as Natalie called it, one of the most common members of the family *Delphinidae*. This one weighed about 500 pounds. The Atlantic spotted dolphin, not the bottlenose, was most common to these waters and the subject of the communication research done here. Though some bottlenose dolphins are known to be residents, most are transient in this part of the world.

That could explain the stranding. It was likely a dolphin who wasn't familiar with these waters. As Natalie had said, probably following fish when it got lost. But that answer was too easy. Something else was going on here.

I also Googled what to do for a stranded dolphin. Kerrie seemed to have it well in hand. The dolphin was shaded from the sun and being cooled by the wet towels. The document, *Marine Mammals Ashore: A Field Guide for Strandings*, stressed the importance of tagging the animal while ashore so that observers would have the opportunity to determine whether the animal survived the ordeal and if rescue procedures were effective. This dolphin already had a satellite transmitter mounted on a molded plastic saddle attached to its dorsal fin. So, regardless of whether it was from this area, its future travels would be documented.

There were unique marks under the pectoral fins that seemed odd to me. I made a mental note to ask Kerrie about those, too. Or maybe Natalie because Kerrie didn't seem to like sharing information. Odd behavior for a researcher.

Finally, Ralph, a local craftsman, arrived with a stretcher for the dolphin made of canvas attached to two poles with holes cut for the dolphin's flippers. The tide was coming in. Apparently, they intended to carry the dolphin into the deeper water.

With Kerrie giving the orders, the men gathered around the dolphin. They seemed to be trying to slide the stretcher under the animal.

"Why don't they roll the dolphin onto the stretcher?" I asked Natalie. "Wouldn't that be easier?"

She shook her head. "For whatever reasons, dolphins don't like being rolled. It might thrash and hurt someone. This way is better. If this doesn't work, they might have to drag it by the fluke."

They managed to get the stretcher under it. Then they gathered, two on each end of a pole.

"At the count of three," Kerrie said. "One, two, three." In one fluid movement, they carefully lifted, then, together, shuffled toward the water. Kerrie, Natalie, and I walked with them.

A hush settled over the onlookers, which had grown into a considerable crowd, as they watched in anticipation.

One step, then another, then another, and we were in the water. I dragged my feet, shuffling along to disturb the sand, trying to avoid catching a stingray by surprise.

"Make sure to keep the head up," Kerrie said. "Don't let the blowhole go under."

As the dolphin started to float, I thought it would kick and buck, then swim away. But it still didn't move much. It seemed to struggle to move at all.

"What's wrong?" I asked Natalie.

"This is normal. It has to acclimate to the water again. It might take hours. Then, sometimes, they need to be towed out to sea because they're still disoriented. This one hasn't been beached long, so let's hope that isn't necessary."

Standing in waist-deep water, the men held the dolphin upright, making sure the blowhole stayed above the surface, and gently rocked the animal from side to side.

"The rocking helps restore blood circulation," Natalie explained.

After about twenty minutes, the dolphin suddenly came to life, squirming against the stretcher.

This was the critical moment, when we'd learn if all our work paid off, if the dolphin would swim away on its own, back out to sea, unharmed.

The dolphin gave a little kick, then slapped its fluke on the water, making a big splash that doused the men. With another slap, it pushed free of the stretcher and swam away, disappearing underwater.

We waited, watching to see if it would be all right. Natalie had said there was a chance it could seize from shock. I looked from Natalie to Kerrie. Natalie watched with anticipation. Kerrie held one hand over her mouth, hugging herself with the other. She seemed worried, like a mother watching her child be taken away in an ambulance.

A moment later, the dolphin surfaced, blowing spray into the air.

The crowd cheered. Kerrie let out a puff of air, her shoulders slumping in relief.

I watched for a little longer and then headed for shore with a big smile on my face. I glanced over to see Dalton smiling back at me.

CHAPTER 2

Kerrie was exhausted. I was exhausted.

"C'mon," Natalie volunteered. "I'll drop you at your room." My suitcase was still strapped to the back of Kerrie's golf cart. My first day on Bimini had been intense and I was ready for a shower and bed.

"Go ahead and take her in my cart, then come back for me," Kerrie said and we were on our way.

The island is so narrow, for most of its seven miles, you can see water on either side—the Atlantic side on one, the bay ringed by mangroves on the other. We passed signs for Porgy Bay, Bailey Town, Alice Town—all in a short couple of miles. Along the shoreline, an occasional old boat lay on its side, thrown up on the beach by some hurricane and left there to the elements. Mounds of trash lay beside houses and restaurants amid the palm trees. Old cars were left to rust in the sun.

On the ride earlier, I'd been struck by the dramatic difference in the north end of the island compared to the south. At the north, rows of look-alike condos with manicured landscaping surrounded a six-story building, all bright white and glistening glass.

"Is that a Hilton?" I asked Natalie.

"With a casino," she responded, the words laced with fake excitement.

"Right," I said. "It fits on this gorgeous tropical island like a two-carat cubic zirconia ring would look on Jane Goodall's hand."

That made Natalie smirk. "I guess it depends on who you ask. The high-speed ferry keeps showing up from Miami full of people. Five hundred a day. They seem to like it."

"I heard they destroyed acres of mangroves to build it and a golf course. That's a tragedy."

"Yeah. If only that was all. But that was just the beginning. For years, well, since the days of Hemingway, the people of this beautiful island have resisted big tourism. Sure, my father made his living from the wealthy American tourists who'd come to dive the pristine reefs and big game fishermen who'd arrive by private yacht or chartered seaplanes. But he understood that his livelihood depended on the sparkling clear waters and white sand beaches.

"Then this Malaysian company shows up one day and somehow got approval to bring 500,000 tourists a year to our tiny island. 500,000 to an island that is seven miles long. The traffic has damaged the coral reefs and the mangroves beyond repair. And they're not stopping. Now they're dredging channels to start bringing in cruise ships. It's caused a big division among us islanders. My dad hasn't spoken to my uncle in years."

I shook my head.

"Some people are short-sighted. All they see are new jobs at the resort. They don't see the big picture." She went on. "The loss of the reef and mangroves will really hurt Bimini in the long run. It's critical habitat for juvenile lobster, grouper, and conch, not to mention a natural storm protection for the island itself."

"And once it's gone, it can never be replaced," I said.

"Same for the livelihood of the locals. All these small, family-owned gift shops and restaurants thought they'd get the benefit of the tourists. But that resort is an all-inclusive deal. No one leaves the property to spend any dollars. Most have had to board up their windows."

"That's tragic," I said, not sure what else to say.

"It's worse. And here's where I get really fired up." She brought the golf cart to a halt to pick up a beer bottle that had been left in the middle of the road. She tossed it in a basket on the back of the cart and continued on. "These waters are home to a huge range of marine animals. The endangered great hammerhead shark lives here. Loggerhead turtles. Queen conch and Caribbean spiny lobster. And of course, the Atlantic spotted dolphins.

"We have to preserve this island habitat. Not just to continue to attract the right kind of tourists, but the whole ecosystem sustains local lifestyles in other ways. But that"—she gestured over her shoulder toward the resort, a scowl on her face—"has put it all at risk."

"I don't understand why it was allowed."

"A few years ago, some local leaders, my father being one of them, wrote to the prime minister, urging him to approve a plan for a marine reserve around North Bimini. He wouldn't do it. Said Bahamians want jobs, not some fish. Instead, the government gave the resort permission for a $150 million upgrade." She frowned. "They just don't get it."

"You've lived here your whole life?"

"I grew up here. But I got to go to college in the States. A lot of my relatives have never been off the island. They're the ones with no options."

"Right," I said.

We arrived at my temporary home—a room on the backside of an old hotel, built circa. 1965.

I retrieved my suitcase and followed Natalie to my room.

"Sorry to be so negative," she said as she opened the door for me. "Not the best first impression, I suppose."

"No, it's okay," I said. "I get it. I can't imagine how

frustrating it is."

"Well, this is it. It's not much, but…"

The fluorescent light flickered to life. On the far side of the room was a mini-fridge and a cart with a one-burner hot plate. A brown stain covered a corner of the linoleum floor. The bed, though, had what looked like a brand new cover and was crisply made. It reminded me of an apartment my dad and I had lived in for a couple months in the Philippines.

"It's great," I said.

She warned me about leaving any food out and to manage the trash or I'd get sugar ants, then said good night. "If you're all set, I'll see you tomorrow."

"All good," I said, shut the door behind her, and collapsed on the bed.

If that hotel and casino project had stirred up that much trouble, was it also somehow related to the problem with the dolphins?

My eyes refused to stay open. I'd have to think about it some more tomorrow when the rest of the team was scheduled to arrive.

Dawn came early. I had several hours before I was to meet Kerrie at her office, so I decided to take a walk. I needed to think, to sort out all the information I'd taken in yesterday.

My room was on the southwest part of the island, so I strolled down the beach and rounded the tip where there were no houses and stood looking out at the sea. Waves crashed onto the beach with that familiar, primal rumble. The fresh salt air and gentle breeze coming off the ocean made me feel alive. I needed this. Especially after my recent bout with the frigid Canadian wilderness.

But this wasn't a vacation. I had to figure out what was going on. *Go see what's happening, if anything, with the dolphins down there.* What kind of directive was that? Dalton and I had recently been assigned to the task force, and Ms. Hyland was our new supervisor. I still hadn't quite figured her out. At first, I'd thought maybe this assignment was her way of giving us a little time off. Tom and Mike had been on a six month sting operation and Dalton and I had come off of a couple of intense operations when we'd joined the team. We were all a little burned out. We don't have a home base, so why not send us to the tropics for a few weeks to recharge our batteries?

But that hadn't seemed plausible, really.

The mission was frustratingly vague. It reminded me of those times when my mother would use the old because-I-said-so line. So aggravating. At least parents could get away with that tactic since children were dependent, had no recourse. But this was an operation and we were professionals. Sure, fresh eyes can be important, but I felt like we were going in blind.

All I knew for sure, was that a dolphin had stranded the day I arrived. It couldn't be a coincidence. Somehow, it was related to whatever was *happening with the dolphins* here.

If my dad were still alive, he would say I should trust my intuition. *You've got a good head on your shoulders,* he used to tell me. *Use it.* I would. If I had somewhere to start.

I dug my feet deep down into the sand to find the cool earth beneath as I watched a crab do that side walk-crawl thing they do along the base of a rock.

Investigating Kerrie was as good a place to start as any. She hadn't exactly been forthcoming with information. And she'd cut off Natalie's sentences. It could have been her stress. But maybe she had something to hide.

Her office was as she'd described, tucked away in a tiny corner of a small research building, but I managed to find it. The six by eight foot room sported wood paneling, hung in the sixties, with one window, half the glass removed for an air conditioner.

"Natalie will be busy all day with follow up from the stranding yesterday," she said, shuffling papers around and clearing off the chair. "And after I stop by and check on a dog who's got some kind of ear infection, I've got to make a report to the board. I'll work on it at home so you can use the computer here. I've got a simple project for you to start with today, but we'll get you out with the dolphins soon, in the water with them."

"No problem," I said, but couldn't help feeling disappointed. "So, tomorrow maybe?"

"Yes. The weather is good. And the guide boat is going out. We don't have our own research vessel. We team up with a local guide who takes snorkelers to swim with the dolphins. He runs SCUBA trips in the morning, then dolphin tours in the afternoon. It's a good partnership because we get a ride and his customers like to have a researcher on board to ask questions."

I smiled. That meant I'd be on the same boat as Dalton. For the case, it was best to split up, glean as much information as possible by working separately. But, hey, if our roles happened to overlap, so be it.

Being close to Dalton was a risk. I needed to make a decision. He was my partner and we'd gotten too close. Way too close. It had affected our performance and, in a couple situations, put us in danger. Not to mention, fraternization was forbidden in the agency. Especially among partners. I suppose that was why. Letting your guard down, even for a moment, in this job could get you killed. The answer was clear. I had to forget about him. He was simply off limits.

But then again, really, what was the big deal? So we cared about each other… aren't partners *supposed* to care about each other? We had a bond. Facing those dangerous situations together helped us build trust, a connection. It was natural.

Dalton had made his opinion of the fraternization rule, and

any other issues I brought up, very clear. To hell with them. But he wasn't clear on how he felt about me, exactly.

I still couldn't decide if it was worth the risk. I'd been working toward this point in my career my whole life. And, for all I knew, this could be one of those relationship situations where you're drawn together simply because your lives are in danger. That didn't mean it was a real bond. Once we weren't partners anymore, we probably wouldn't even be compatible.

But my god he was hot. And kind. And he seemed to really dig me.

Maybe I should've taken my best friend Chris's advice and gone ahead and had sex with Dalton. Get it over with. Break the sexual tension, let off all the steam, as he'd put it. It was probably all the teasing and flirting that was distracting me. Yeah, just go ahead. It would probably actually help the situation.

No. Dalton was my partner. That was it. That was all it was going to be.

But the way he kissed, and that body, wow, could he wear a pair of jeans, he and I would—

"Are you with me?" Kerrie said.

Visions of Dalton vanished. I nodded. I had a job to do.

The project Kerrie assigned was to sort through hundreds of photographs taken of dorsal fins above water, categorize those that were out of focus or otherwise unrecognizable, then match the recognizable ones to dolphins that had already been identified. If not, put them in another folder for future identification.

"I'm not sure what you mean by matching," I said.

"The dorsal fins are unique, kinda like a fingerprint. They have nicks and sometimes even shark bites. As you sort through, you start to recognize certain animals. You'll see."

She moved to leave.

"Did you say you've got to check on a dog?"

"Yeah, on my way home."

"So you *are* a veterinarian?" Natalie had said she wasn't. That's why she'd called the network for help.

"No. But I'm the best they've got on the island. I do basic stuff between the visits from the vet who comes from Nassau once or twice a year."

"Oh, I see."

"I've really got to go," she said and swept out the door, assuring me we'd do something more fun tomorrow. Maybe she was trying to make up for her coolness toward me yesterday. I still didn't trust her. Something was definitely up.

Once she left, I sent a text to my team, letting them know we needed to meet tonight for an update.

We met on Tom and Mike's fishing boat, which was in the marina not far from my room, so we could talk inside the cabin, away from any onlookers.

Though I'd been on the task force for a few months now, I was still getting to know Tom. On our first op together, in our undercover roles, we hadn't crossed paths much, but he'd been a solid guy—polite, very professional. He might or might not have an inkling that Dalton and I had feelings for each other. I wasn't sure what to do about that. So far, he'd been cool.

Mike, on the other hand, had a hot Italian temper and an unpredictable, loose-cannon style. I wasn't sure how I'd feel about seeing him again. He had been my partner on our first operation together and things hadn't gone so well. The fact is, I'd learned a hard lesson about ambition and deceit. While I can't call him a friend, I do have to work with him. I'll never turn my back on him again, though.

They'd commandeered a forty-eight foot fishing yacht in Miami from the government shipyard, one that had been repossessed, probably for drug smuggling or tax evasion or something nefarious, and driven the fifty-some miles, through the night, across the Gulf Stream.

Maybe Tom was being influenced by Mike's method-acting attitude because, not only did they take their undercover roles seriously and dressed for the part—Tom had on a button-down Guy Harvey shirt with tan Bermuda shorts and flip-flops, Mike wore a T-shirt with a marlin splashed with paint in red, green, and yellow, gray shorts and sandals—but they seemed so relaxed, I wondered if they'd notice if an aircraft carrier pulled into the harbor.

Dalton and I sat next to each other, across from them, in the tiny dinette. Sitting so close to him made me feel nervous. How silly. We'd been partners now for over a year. I trusted him with my life. There was nothing to be nervous about. Yet my heartbeat picked up and my mouth felt a little dry. He was just so…mmmm… Dalton smelled like the sea and soap and an indescribable masculinity that left me wanting to bury my nose in that spot where his neck meets his shoulder and maybe trail my lips up to his ear...

Concentrate. "You two like the boat?" I asked.

Tom shrugged.

Mike swigged a beer. "Not the smell. It's only a few years old, but still, somehow, it reeks of salt, mildew, and fish guts."

"Yes, but this boat so perfectly fits your cover as obnoxious fishermen," I said.

"How so?" Tom asked, all innocent.

"Seriously? It's called *Droppin' Skirts.*"

"What? Skirts are a kind of fishing lure…thing," he grinned.

"Oh, gimme a break," I rolled my eyes.

Mike said, "Our timing is right on. There's a big wahoo fishing tournament this week."

"What's a wahoo?"

They both shrugged.

Tom smiled wider. "Don't worry, we're studying."

"Well, you wouldn't be the first men ever to buy a big fishing boat and not know which end of the pole to stick in the water."

Dalton ignored our banter. "I met the dive team today. Nice folks. Got the rundown on daily excursions. Nothing out of the ordinary. I asked about interaction with the dolphins. They seemed pretty strict about the rules for their protection." He turned to me and I felt myself flush. "I got nothing else."

Stay on the task, McVie. "Well, I have some interesting info. I don't know if you heard, but yesterday, when I arrived, we went straight to the north end of the island, because a dolphin had stranded on the beach."

Mike and Tom looked surprised.

"No kidding?" said Tom.

"What are the odds?" I said.

"What'd the researcher say about it?" Dalton asked.

"That's just it. She was hard to read. It was pretty stressful for her, which I'm sure is normal. But I got the feeling she didn't want to share much. Her assistant started to say something, a couple times, and she cut her off. I got the impression that wasn't her normal manner."

Tom leaned in. "Do you think she's hiding something?"

"I don't know. She did seem…tight lipped. But I have a hard time imagining it's because she's up to something criminal." I turned to Dalton. "I did find out that she doesn't have a boat of her own. We'll be going out on your dive boat with you." I grinned.

If he was happy about that, he revealed nothing. Typical Dalton. Not a flicker. That's why he was so good undercover. "Yeah, I wondered about that," he muttered, seeming to be pondering the implications.

"I know it's not ideal. But it's the situation. And sometimes, in the same scenario, we might see different things." I nodded, trying to assure my team it wouldn't be a big deal.

"Yeah, no. I've been thinking." Dalton turned to the guys. "Are you two comfortable with this boat? It's kinda big. I mean, maybe, Tom, I know you're SCUBA certified. Maybe you'd prefer to move over to the divemaster job? I can captain for Mike."

The wind left my sails. What was he doing? Didn't he want to work with me?

Tom shrugged. "Whatever you want. I'm not sure that—"

Oh no. No way. "They just drove it over from Miami," I said. "Across the Gulf Stream, no less. I'm sure they know what they're doing. What is this about?"

Dalton held my gaze for a moment too long. "Nothing. I don't know. I just thought—I get to dive all day. It seems too good to be true." He smirked. "Just trying to share the love."

CHAPTER 3

It was dark when we left the boat and Dalton moved to walk me to my room.

"You don't have to do that," I said. I needed some space to sort out why he'd reacted the way he did, why he didn't want to work with me on the dolphin boat everyday.

"I know. But I want to," he said. "Besides, it's not safe."

"Not safe? This is Bimini. And I can take care of myself anyway." I was a trained federal agent, after all. And an expert street fighter, besides.

"I know. I just…"

"You just what?"

"I just want you to be able to relax, enjoy being here. You've been under a lot of stress lately and—"

"And you haven't?"

He took me by the hand. "Let's walk along the beach."

I pulled my hand away. "What if someone sees us?"

"What if they do?" He took my hand in his again and held it tightly. "There's no reason anyone seeing us together can't think we're lovers on this op."

"What?" I spun on him, met his eyes. "A few minutes ago, you didn't want to be near me."

He shifted backward on his heels, leaning away from me, a look of surprise on his face. "What are you talking about?"

"What am I talking about?" *What the hell?* "You were trying to switch roles with Tom so you don't have to be on the boat with me."

"Well, yeah. That's what you keep telling me, that we can't work together. Isn't it?"

I stared at him. It was true. I had said that...but—"Well, yeah, but—"

"But nothing." He crossed his arms. "You've been really clear on the matter."

"Yes, but—"

"You can't have it both ways."

God, he was so infuriating.

He looked at me with those heart-melting eyes. "I can handle it though. Can you?"

He was challenging me. Were we denying our feelings? Or was he saying he could handle being in a relationship with me and work together? Maybe he thinks it's worth the risk.

How the hell do I ask that?

"You know I can handle anything that gets thrown at me," I said. "I can roll with it. I'm the queen of rolling with it."

He was grinning at me. A wicked grin.

"What?"

"Nothing."

"What?"

"You don't know what you want, do you?"

I know I want you. "I know when things are complicated. And you should, too."

"Okay," he said and started walking again, taking me by the hand and tugging me along after him.

Once we were on the beach—the same spot I'd stood earlier—where the waves now caressed the sand in slow, rhythmic pulses, he turned, took my other hand in his, and faced me.

"Listen," he said. "I'm here. Right here. One way or the other. Whatever you decide. But I do wish you'd decide."

Did he mean… I took a deep breath, steadying myself. I was in control. "Well, you know it's complicated and—"

"I don't care. I can handle complicated. Especially for something I want." His eyes held mine.

"You want?" The sand below my feet began to shift.

He didn't blink, didn't look away.

"Well, I—"

"Unless you've got some other argument. Perhaps some new information for me to ponder." He was teasing me now.

"Ponder? You?" I teased back.

"If you ask me, I think you've been doing too much pondering." He wrapped his hands around my waist, setting my nerves buzzing. "Too much thinking. Over thinking." He pulled me to him. My heartbeat picked up. I was in his arms, pressed against him. *Breathe.* "Not enough feeling." His lips were inches from mine. "Kiss me," he said, his voice low.

My breath caught in my throat. "What? I really think—"

"Shut up and kiss me."

His lips met mine, warm and intoxicating. My lips parted and the touch of his tongue on mine sent an electric sizzle down my spine. He kissed me slowly at first, then with more intensity, hungering for more. My whole body flushed with warmth. Somehow, he knew just how to kiss me, how to get my insides to melt.

"We shouldn't…" I whispered between kisses.

He pressed his lips to my ear. His breath, hot on my skin— "Oh, we definitely should. We're here. In the tropics. Practically on vacation." He nuzzled my ear.

My fingers were in his hair, tugging at the base of his neck. He smelled so good. And the feel of his skin. The waves lapped on the shore. And the ocean air felt like heaven.

Maybe Chris was right. If we'd just get it over with, let off a little steam… Why not? What was the big deal anyway? It was nobody's business who I slept with. Not my mom's. Not my boss's. And this was Dalton.

He ran his hand down my back side and drew me tighter to him, pulling me up against his hard body. *Yes, let off a little steam.* I kissed him with new vigor. I wanted so badly to let go. To enjoy it.

I was standing on the edge of a cliff, dizzy with the urge to jump.

My nerves started to buzz again.

It's just sex. Don't read so much into it. Have a good time.

But that would be too impulsive. Irresponsible. Too…

Oh hell. Screw that.

I pressed against him and he responded with a passion I hadn't felt from him before. It was as if he couldn't get enough. His hand came around to my breast. I drew in a quick breath.

"Oh, Poppy," he moaned as his hands moved lower.

"Maybe we should take this back to my room," I said.

He pulled away, looked me in the eyes. "Are you sure?"

I nodded. *Yes.* I decided. And suddenly I felt free. Gloriously free. And certain. It wasn't reckless abandon, but knowing exactly what I wanted and going after it.

He took my hand, spun me around, and tugged me toward the hotel like the beach was on fire. Nothing was going to keep him from getting us there. He was a force of nature and the vortex of his passion drew me after him.

At my door, I fumbled with the key. Dalton had the good sense not to help me with it.

Once inside, we didn't even turn on a light. In an instant, we resumed the position we'd been in on the beach, my body tight against his, my hands in his hair, his hands moving all over my body.

"You drive me out of my mind," he said, passion in his voice.

"Yeah?" I said, pulling back a little. I pulled my top over my head, then unclipped my bra and flung it across the room.

"How about now?"

With a guttural moan, he gathered me in his arms and gently placed me on the bed. He stared at me in the dim, orange light from the streetlight outside my window as he took his time unbuttoning his shirt.

"Hurry up," I said, worried I sounded like I was afraid I'd change my mind. Or he would.

"Oh no. I'm going to enjoy every delicious moment."

I bit my lip. He stood before me, unzipping his shorts, his eyes locked onto mine, a look on his face that confirmed his words—he wanted to savor the moment.

He dropped his shorts to the floor, stepped out of them, and lowered himself onto the bed next to me.

I couldn't take it. We'd put this off for too long. I rolled over on top of him, straddling him at the waist.

"I'm on top," I said.

"Of course," he whispered. "But what's your hurry?"

"Are you kidding? You broke a land speed record on the way here from the beach."

"Yeah. I wanted to get your clothes off before you changed your mind. But now that I have…" His eyes traveled down my body, then back up. He reached up, took a strand of my hair and ran it through his fingers. "We've got all night."

His hands splayed across my shoulder and slowly ran down the side of my arms.

Sparks shot through me. Furious and erratic. "I told you yes," I said as I ran my fingers across his muscular chest. His chest hair was damp with sweat. I leaned forward, letting my hair graze his skin as I slowly bent over him, hoping it would drive him crazy. "Don't make me wait any longer," I breathed into his ear.

He resisted, only a moment, to whisper. "You're sure?"

I nodded.

He kissed me softly, gently, as his hands moved to encircle

me. Then, in an instant, he had me fully enveloped in his arms as he rolled us over and ended up on top of me.

I let a giggle escape.

"God, you're so hot," he moaned. "And you still have too many clothes on." He worked at the zipper on my shorts.

I wanted to pull them off, be the one taking charge, but it felt so good to be seduced.

After a bit of fumbling, he'd slid them off, and his own boxers, and held himself erect over me in the dim light, looking down at me. With those eyes.

Then he was kissing me again, drugging me with his slow, butter-melting kisses that left me panting. But this time, he didn't stop. The intensity built until I couldn't focus, couldn't think.

Just feel.

Until, in the heat of the night, I lost all control.

CHAPTER 4

I awoke in a groggy haze of contentment.

Dalton lay beside me. When I moved, he wrapped his arms around me and pulled me tight. "Let's do that every night," he whispered.

"And twice on Sundays," I said before I could catch the words from escaping my mouth.

Oh no. I recognized the feelings. All the warm fuzzies and soft shivers. I thought for sure he'd slink out the door. Or I'd want to. I'd been counting on it. Easier to avoid all the awkwardness that way.

What do I do with this?

"I can't believe you made me wait so long, but, oh my—" he kissed me on my neck "—you were worth the wait."

I smiled. My cheeks flushed pink.

"God, you're so beautiful."

"You already got me into bed. You don't have to keep up with the compliments," I said dryly.

He pulled away and pushed himself up onto his elbow. "What? Is that what you think?" He looked hurt. "I've just been trying to get you into bed?"

"Well, no. Well, yeah, but no."

He shook his head. "You are something. I don't even know right now if I should be insulted or what."

"No," I said, regretting my words. "It's me. Really." *How'd*

I screw this up already? "That's not what I meant."

"Well, what did you mean?"

What did I mean? "I just…you're always…"

"You need to learn how to take a compliment." He seemed satisfied with his conclusion.

"You're right," I said. "That's it. That's all."

He kissed me on my forehead, rolled out of bed, and got dressed. "I gotta get to work. I'll see you this afternoon on the boat."

"Yeah." I wrapped the sheet around me and headed into my bathroom. The fluorescent light flickered to life and I stared at my reflection in the rusty mirror.

"Oh crap," I said to the woman facing me. "What were you thinking? Now everything will change."

Maybe I should call Chris.

God no. The last thing I needed was more advice from him.

Chris was my best friend. He'd been the one to encourage this relationship. But he'd never understand. He'd give up anything for love.

I shook my head. *Nope. Not calling him.* I knew what he'd say. *We love who we love.* All that crap.

But this wasn't love anyway. Simple case of lust taking over my brain. It had just been too long, that's all. Work had been crazy. I'd almost gotten killed a couple times recently. I needed a little release. That's all.

To the reflection, I said, "Don't make more of it than what it is."

I couldn't think about this now.

After a quick shower, I stepped into some shorts and a tank top and was off to work.

Kerrie had me sorting fin photos again. Not exactly the kind of work to keep your mind off things. What had I been thinking? I should not have done that. But, omigod, wow.

I knew that man could kiss, but, yikes. My head was still spinning, the two sides at odds. My logical brain said, stop this right now. The other part of my brain couldn't focus at all, thinking only of his body and mine, together. Whew.

And now, right after lunch, I'd be on the dive boat, and expected to focus, to learn more about the dolphins, pay attention and watch for criminals. But I'd be there with Dalton. I caught my breath. Yeah, this was bad.

Get a grip. Like he said, we can have sex as much as we want. In our undercover roles, we could play lovers. No problem. It wasn't a big deal. And people managed the friends-with-benefits thing all the time.

At one thirty, Natalie stopped by the office to pick up the video equipment and we headed for the marina together.

As we walked down the dock toward the boat, I noticed Dalton and the captain were already on board. I drew in a breath and steeled myself. *Act normal.*

"Ooooh, so that's the new divemaster," Natalie said with a mischievous grin. "He's nice on the eyes."

My jaw muscles tightened. I needed to get ahead of this. "Yeah, we, uh, met yesterday, on the beach, and kinda hit it off."

Her eyebrows shot up. "Really?"

"I mean, who knows if anything—"

"No need to say more," she said with a knowing grin. "I've got the message."

Kerrie came up behind us with more gear. "Are you ready?" she asked me.

"Sure am," I said.

We carried the gear on board the dive boat and Natalie showed me where it gets stowed.

Dalton introduced himself to Kerrie and Natalie.

"And good afternoon to you," he said to me with a wink.

I blushed twelve shades of red. *What the hell? Get it together,*

McVie.

Captain Ron, a man in his late forties with sun-weathered skin, thinning hair tied back into a ponytail, and a mustache in dire need of a trim, was at the helm. We pulled away from the slip to move the boat around to another dock where the snorkelers waited to be picked up.

"Are you excited?" Dalton whispered to me.

I nodded.

"Me too. I can't wait for tonight." He buried his face in my hair and found my ear. "We should skip dinner and go right to dessert."

Something fluttered around in my stomach like a damn butterfly. I couldn't respond.

"You all right?" he asked, concern in his eyes.

"Yeah, of course." I gave him a little shrug.

"You just…" He frowned. "You're not alright."

"I'm fine. What could be wrong?"

The boat nudged the dock fenders. Dalton moved away from me to toss the line around the post. As soon as he had it tied, he turned back to me. "We should talk."

"I'm fine," I said and gave him a big smile. I was. Really.

The boat held seats for twelve snorkelers, plus room for the crew. The sunburned tourists filed onboard, one at a time and found their seats.

"Oh my gosh! I can't believe it." A female voice.

I swung around. A woman, my age, maybe a little older, with long, straight dark hair and strikingly-beautiful eyes stared at Dalton with her mouth hanging open. One hand dropped to her belly—she must have been about seven months pregnant— while the other nudged her husband.

The man looked right at Dalton. "Sumbitch. Dalton. I didn't know you were working here in The Bahamas."

"Yeah, yeah," Dalton said with his usual calm demeanor. But this could be a problem—people who knew him from real life, or worse, a previous op. "Yeah, I'm a divemaster now."

The woman shook her head with confusion. "I thought you were—"

"No, that didn't really work out."

She looked even more confused. Obviously, she knew Dalton personally, but didn't seem to understand that he might be undercover.

Dalton looked at her, down at her belly. "I see you're—" His eyes snapped back to her husband. "I didn't know you two were…together."

"Yeah, I, uh, tried to call you, but, uh, couldn't catch up with you. You know, we kinda lost touch."

Dalton nodded, a little more than normal.

The woman stared at Dalton in a curious way.

"Honey, let's not hold things up," the man said to his wife, urging her to a seat. "Sit down there. We've got the whole boat ride to catch up."

I came up beside Dalton before they could step away. "Old friends?" I asked.

He lowered his voice. "Rod's a SEAL. I've known him since boot camp."

"Ah," I nodded to Rod in greeting. He looked like a SEAL. Similar build as Dalton. Fit. Big arms. "Nice to meet you."

I looked to the woman. She offered her hand. "And I'm Alison. Dalton's ex-wife."

Uh, what? Wife?

I stared at her. Had no words. No undercover training had prepared me to hide my reaction.

She looked from me to Dalton, then back to me. "Oh, so you two are a couple?" She grinned with the knowledge.

"Did you say wife?" My eyes snapped to Dalton's.

He shifted his stance. "You know, right now is probably not the time—"

Saved by the Captain. He hushed the crowd, asking everyone

to get seated, then gave a quick overview of the location of life jackets and other safety features before we pulled away from the dock.

I hoped I wouldn't need that information because I didn't hear a word of it.

Married. Dalton never mentioned having been married. He never said anything about an ex-wife. Did he? No, I would have remembered that. Should I have asked? I don't know. Seems like something you'd include in conversations sometime *before* sex. Maybe?

An ex-wife. And now, married to an old friend. And pregnant.

I watched him for any sign of what he was feeling. I'm not sure why; Dalton never gave his feelings away. He could hide anything. That's what made him so good at this job. He'd take a secret to his grave. Of that, I was sure.

Me, well, I was still working on that skill. Everything I'm thinking seems to play out on my face, at least when it comes to personal issues.

I couldn't help staring at her. She was stunning. Long dark hair and hazel-green eyes. She had the legs of a dancer and perfect skin. Definitely the kind of woman you'd expect on Dalton's arm. Unlike me, with my crazy, do-whatever-it-wants hair and my boyish figure. And she had a glow about her. Some women, when pregnant, get that look of misery, as though every movement pains them. Her rosy cheeks and pleasant smile made her seem utterly content, as though her most joyous contribution to the world was to bear beautiful babies.

Is that what Dalton wanted? A child? He'd never mentioned it. We'd never talked about that at all. Marriage. A family. Kids. Was he hurting right now seeing her pregnant? And with an old friend?

I never thought of him that way. A dad. Until yesterday. And then I'd learned he had two siblings. Something else I didn't know about him.

My stomach twisted into a weird shape. A shape of worry. Had she crushed his heart? Was that why he was so aloof? So…the Dalton I thought I knew.

Or had he hurt her? I suddenly felt like I didn't know him at all.

I tried not to stare. At her or him.

But I noticed, as we rounded the buoy at the end of the harbor, that he casually walked by, leaned into her, and whispered in her ear. He was probably telling her he was undercover, to be careful with her questions. Would he reveal that? She was his ex-wife, after all. Certainly telling her was a better option than letting her blow our cover. She obviously wasn't involved with whatever was going on with the dolphins here. She and Rod could be informed of his need for secrecy without compromising the op. Assuming they'd respect his situation.

Natalie came up beside me and whispered, "Well, that was awkward."

I shrugged. "No matter. I hardly know him."

"Right," she said. "But still."

I busied myself helping the other passengers fit their masks and fins as we headed out to sea.

Kerrie hung onto the back of the Captain's chair and addressed the group over the rumble of the engine as the boat moved through the waves.

"So, who here has ever seen a dolphin before?"

A few hands went up.

"In the wild?"

The hands went down.

"I guarantee, this will be an experience like no other. I'm excited to share it with you today. Though of course, I must be clear. These are wild animals and wild animals don't always cooperate."

Kinda like children, I thought.

"Hopefully we'll find some today and they'll be in a playful mood. I want to start with a little overview about dolphins and dolphin behavior. You might not know, but dolphins are mammals, just like us. They're warm-blooded, breathe air, and have live young, which they nurse, and they even have some hair."

This brought some surprised looks around the group of faces.

"Dolphins are toothed-whales. But their teeth aren't like ours. They have a single row of teeth that are all alike. They mainly use them for grabbing fish, not chewing.

"Does anyone know the land animal who's the closest living relative to dolphins?"

"Land?" someone said.

"Believe it or not, it's the hippopotamus." That brought more surprised looks. "The dolphins we know of today have existed in their current form for about five million years. As they evolved, their front limbs became flippers." She held up her own arm as an example. "They have the same bones in those flippers as we have in our arms and hands."

"How fast can they swim?" someone asked.

"They can swim as fast as twenty-five miles per hour in bursts," she said. "They move through the water using a single muscular peduncle, that's the long part of the tail, and their flukes work like a paddle.

"Today, we are most likely to see the Atlantic spotted dolphin, but we may come across some bottlenose dolphins. Here in Bimini, the spotted dolphins are more easily approached and tolerant of our presence in the water."

One woman raised her hand, looking worried. "I've heard that dolphins are known to rape people."

I stared at the woman in disbelief. Was she serious?

Kerrie clearly had encountered this myth before. "There's no need to worry. We've never had any kind of incident in the wild that would suggest any truth in that. I'm sure that idea has been perpetuated by the many swim programs, where captive dolphins are forced to interact with the participants in ways that are counter to their natural behavior, particularly the popular activity of women wanting selfies with the dolphins. That kind of close contact can be aggravating for them and they can become quite upset. But rape behavior, that's just not…" She shook her head.

"I have a question." It was Alison, the *ex-wife*, her hand in the air. "What are the threats to these dolphins? I mean, are they healthy here?"

"That's a good question," Kerrie said. "This is a healthy population, as far as we can tell. In the years we've been studying this group, they've shown a normal birth and mortality rate, and their overall body conditions are good."

That was interesting. If the scientists considered this community of dolphins healthy, why were we here? The stranding incident was obviously a problem, but that was typically a rare occurrence and probably didn't need to be mentioned to a bunch of tourists. But she could be lying about the overall health of the dolphin population to keep the tourists coming. Mental note: follow up on that one.

"The biggest threat is noise in the ocean," she went on. "These animals are highly sensitive to sound. The main way they experience the world and understand their surroundings is by the use of echolocation. They send out sound waves and read the echoes to visualize, or perceive, the three-dimensional world. Their ability to do this is absolutely astounding. Their perception is incredibly accurate. Not only can they determine shapes in space, they can also identify the substance. For example, whether it's made of rock or metal."

"But can they talk to each other?" someone else asked.

"Well, that's the main focus of our research here. What we know for sure, is that they are able to communicate with each other. Whether they use a *language*, as defined in the traditional way, is yet to be determined. Natalie, my research assistant"—Natalie gave the group a wave—"has also been studying their interactions and determining relationships. We are establishing the family tree, so to speak."

Alison piped up again. "You're able to cross match DNA samples?"

"Oh, no," Kerrie said, shaking her head. "Our study here is noninvasive. We never touch the dolphins for anything. All our data are collected through visual observation. We've been at it long enough to connect mothers and calves, so maternal lineage, and then we track their social relationships."

"Off the starboard bow," the Captain shouted.

Kerrie swung around. "How many?"

"Ten, maybe twelve."

She grinned. "Get your masks on."

CHAPTER 5

"Okay, everyone. Please remember rule number one: absolutely *do not* touch the dolphins. Their skin is extremely sensitive. They don't like it. Also, if we see anyone chasing a dolphin, we'll pull you out of the water. Got it?"

Heads nodded as the tourists, clad in brightly-colored fins and masks, plopped into the water off the stern, two at a time. Kerrie scowled. She'd made a point of asking people to gently enter the water.

Natalie toted the video gear and told me to go ahead and enjoy my first experience without worrying about the equipment.

I admit, I was thrilled by her generous offer, and anxious to be with the dolphins.

Dolphins had always been a favorite animal of mine. As a child, they seemed like magical, mythical beings and had a grip on my imagination. Though some so-called-scientists claim they are no more intelligent than dogs, which are pretty darn intelligent, I say we can't accurately assess such a thing. At least not until we can agree on the definition of intelligence.

As soon as I was in the water, I put my head under and looked around. The indigo blue world shimmered with shafts of sunlight that streaked across the sandy bottom. Two dolphins shot by, swimming on their sides with their bellies facing me. They zoomed by so fast, I almost missed them.

Amid the gurgle of the waves, I could hear their high-pitched clicking as they circled the group of snorkelers. One at a time, they darted through, so agile between the gangly human bodies, as though it were a fun obstacle course to traverse. They seemed as curious about us as we were of them. They wanted to play, too.

I drew in a long breath and pushed downward, below the surface, and twirled around so I could see all directions. Looking up, the surface looked the same as it does from above—a silvery mirror in constant motion. A young dolphin sped toward me and twirled next to me, matching my spin, in perfect synchronization. I twirled again, this time the other direction, and the dolphin copied my movements. I let out a squeal. The dolphin dove under me, then circled, looking me right in the eyes. For a moment, there was nothing else but me and the dolphin, playing. But I had to surface for a breath.

I kicked downward again, corkscrewing my way to the sandy bottom, but the dolphin was gone.

I kicked and twirled, hoping it would come back, but it was off, zipping around another swimmer. Two more dolphins shot through the center of the group, fast as torpedoes.

Kicking hard, I attempted to lure them in with the twirling routine. Two immediately swirled around me, swimming much faster than I was to keep up with my spin. These must have been juveniles; their bodies weren't as spotted as some of the others. And they seemed a bit smaller. But they swam with an easy grace, their bodies perfectly shaped for their ocean environment.

The way they kept eye contact and moved to stay in perfect sync made me feel as if they wanted to connect, wanted to engage. Their eyes contained an almost human intelligence. Curiosity. Innocence. I imagined they must have been amused by us humans with our awkward arms and googled eyes.

A mother swam close by with a calf at her dorsal fin, a sign that these dolphins were comfortable in the presence of people in the water. Perhaps they viewed us as inept creatures who couldn't do them harm. If only that were true.

I envied their child-like innocence.

Then, with some shared, silent signal, they all vanished.

I came to the surface and looked around for the boat. The captain was waving us back onboard.

After several attempts of sticking my head underneath to scan and seeing nothing while the other swimmers heaved themselves out of the water, I swam to the boat.

Dalton was stationed at the stern. He offered his hand and pulled me out of the water and back onto the boat. "You looked like you were having a good time," he said quietly.

I grinned. I really had. I moved away so he could help other swimmers aboard.

"Where'd the dolphins go?" I asked Kerrie.

She shrugged. "Sometimes they just move on."

Once all the swimmers were back aboard, I moved next to Alison. "Did you enjoy that?" I asked.

"Yes, I guess." She shrugged. "I've loved dolphins my whole life. I've always dreamed of coming here." She raised her leg to show me a tattoo at her ankle—a dolphin, arched in mid-leap. "I've read these accounts where dolphins can sense when someone is pregnant, you know. They hear the baby's heartbeat or use their echolocation or something. And I thought maybe, I don't know, that they'd be attracted to me. Maybe I'd…you know, there'd be a connection." She shrugged again. "I don't know. It was silly, I guess."

"I don't think it was silly," I said.

"It was silly." She sighed in resignation. "To think I could be one who…"

I gave her a smile. "Maybe it was too much to expect of them in the short few minutes we had."

She nodded. "I'm sure you're right."

"So how far along are you?"

She smiled, glowing. "Six months."

I had about five million other questions—about her, about Dalton, about their marriage—but none felt right to form into words and let out of my head.

The others on the boat stirred, alerted by something in the water.

The captain announced that there was another dolphin approaching off the port bow.

The dolphin came right up next to the boat and bobbed in the water, holding itself upright.

"This is the bottlenose dolphin," Kerrie announced to the group, then quietly said to the captain, "Let's move on."

The captain seemed confused by her command, but put the boat in gear.

The dolphin squealed and chomped its jaws as it bobbed up and down.

Was this the same dolphin who had been stranded? It had a satellite transmitter strapped to the dorsal fin, just like the other.

"Looks like he wants a fish," a man said.

The dolphin spun around, then squealed again.

"Is it trying to get our attention for something?" I asked Kerrie.

She hesitated before answering, "It's just curious is all." To the entire group, she said, "Bottlenose dolphins can be quite animated."

"Can we get back in the water?" the same man asked.

"No," Kerrie said with an unexpected harshness. "Like I said, the spotted dolphins are tolerant of our presence, but the bottlenose can be unpredictable. They're larger and stronger, too."

Another woman piped up. "I thought they were the friendly ones."

Kerrie patiently responded. "It's not that they are friendly or unfriendly. Different dolphins in different parts of the world demonstrate different behaviors. For example, here in Bimini, the bottlenose dolphins have a unique feeding technique called crater feeding, which, as far as we know, they don't do anywhere else in the world. They use their echolocation to investigate critters hiding just below the sand. Once they've discovered something of interest, they turn their bodies upside down, drilling their rostrums into the sand and pulling out their treat.

"If we see a group today that is crater feeding, we might be able to get in the water to watch. It's the only time they tolerate us. Otherwise, they flee."

"Except for this one." The woman made it a statement, obviously annoyed by Kerrie's explanation.

"There's always an exception," Kerrie said with a fake smile.

So what was it about *that* dolphin? A dolphin just like the one that was stranded?

After another hour without seeing another dolphin, the boat made a turn, back toward the harbor.

Dalton handed out tropical fruit punch served in paper cups as the captain increased speed.

Back at the dock, Rod and Alison lingered after the other swimmers departed. "Let's get lunch. Catch up," Rod said to Dalton.

"Uh, sure. I just need to get the boat swabbed and stuff locked down. Meet you over at the Bimini Big Game Club bar?"

"Sure, that's where we're staying. See you there."

I gave them a wave and moved next to Dalton. He might be able to hide his emotions well most of the time, but I could sense his discomfort—the way he kept his eyes down, went right for the mop.

"So," I said. "Married?"

He stopped what he was doing, stared at the deck for a full three seconds, then looked up at me. "We shouldn't discuss this right now."

"Okay. But, *married?* You never told me you were married." I tried to hide what I was feeling. What was I feeling? "But Dalton, you and I—" I clammed up. He was right; we shouldn't discuss this right now.

He paused from his mopping long enough to say, "We were young. And it was a Navy marriage. You know how that goes."

I did. I'd grown up a Navy brat and I'd seen marriages crumble under the pressure of long term separation, the long work hours, and the lack of choice in duty stations.

He leaned on the mop and held my gaze. "She wanted a different life."

I nodded. "But Rod? You said he's a SEAL, too."

"Probably didn't re-up."

"I'll ask him."

He started shaking his head. "Oh no—"

"Oh, yes. I'm going." I gave him a wink. "I wouldn't miss that world-famous Bimini Big Game Club bar salad for anything."

The fish stretched twelve feet in length, easily. Two blue marlins. Made of fiberglass. I think. All shiny with gloss, hanging on a wall at the entrance to the Bimini Big Game Club.

Big fish seemed to be the theme around here. Probably since the 1930s, when Hemingway liked to hang out and string up anything he could snag out of the sea—bluefin tuna, blue marlin, swordfish, mako shark. Apparently he'd left quite a mark on the place. His fame brought prosperity in its wake, making Bimini a world-renowned fishing destination. Thankfully, as far as I could tell, he'd left the dolphins alone.

Now, because of him, the quaint resort was a well-known historical landmark. It had a fresh coat of paint—tropical blue and yellow—yet somehow maintained the nostalgia.

Honeymooners strolled by, hand in hand. Kids splashed in the pool and a nice breeze blew in from the harbor.

Rod and Alison had chosen a table for four in the corner of the patio overlooking the marina. Rod rose from his chair as we approached and shook Dalton's hand.

Dalton pulled out the chair for me and placed his hand on my lower back as I moved to sit. In a low voice, he said, "This is my partner, Special Agent Poppy McVie."

I nodded. "Nice to meet you."

Alison looked at me skeptically, then eyed Dalton. "So, you two aren't—"

"We're undercover," Dalton said. "And you two are"—big pause—"on your honeymoon?"

Rod nodded. "Dude, I meant to call you and—"

Dalton held up a hand. "No need, man. We're cool. It's not like you owe me anything." He smiled at Alison. "I'm happy for you. Really, I am."

A smile slowly came to her face and she seemed genuinely relieved.

Dalton gestured toward her belly. "It's what you always wanted."

She nodded as she grasped Rod's hand in hers. "We're gonna move home to Montana. Rod got a job at the post office."

An expression of nostalgia crossed Dalton's face, for a fleeting moment, then it was gone. He was from Montana. Was Alison his high school sweetheart? Made sense. Had they planned to move back home? Start a family?

"Last week, I stopped in to see your mom."

Dalton tensed, made the tiniest shake of his head.

Alison ignored it. "She looks good, I mean, not great, but good. Sarah and I got her to wash her hair. She's difficult but at least she's still got spirit. Sarah said—"

"Not now, Alison." Dalton's eyes flashed with warning.

Alison shrank back in her seat a little and Rod put his hand on her thigh. Clearly these three knew something I didn't. I felt a pang of jealousy. There was something very intimate about knowing someone's past. What did I really even know about Dalton? Hell, it took me forever to find out his first name.

The waitress, a middle-aged black Bahamian woman with a scowl on her face, appeared and they each ordered the famous mahi-mahi sandwich. I asked for a salad and the peas and rice. The guys and I ordered beers. Without acknowledgement, she turned and shuffled toward the kitchen.

"Not very friendly around here, are they?" Rod said.

Alison squeezed his hand and he frowned.

"You have family in Montana?" I asked Alison, picking back up the conversation.

She nodded. "And I've got a job lined up, too. I'm an elementary school teacher."

Dalton—the man who'd brawled with a serial killer last month and barely survived a knife in his thigh—married to an elementary school teacher. That I could not picture. But then again, I hadn't seen this one coming either.

"That sounds just ducky," I said. It didn't sound so ridiculous in my head before it came out of my mouth.

A laughing gull squawked from the rooftop, mocking me.

"Remember the old Johnson farm?" Alison asked Dalton. "We've bought it. Dad's going to help us remodel. And we can lease the land."

"That's nice," Dalton said.

Rod, clearly uncomfortable, cleared his throat. "So, you said you're undercover. What's going on? Are you at liberty to tell us?"

Dalton nodded in acknowledgment. "Our discretion. Poppy and I work for Fish and Wildlife, but we've been assigned to a special task force. We're here to investigate some issues with the dolphins."

"What kind of issues?" Alison asked. "The scientist said there weren't any problems here, that it's a healthy population. Is that not true?"

"We're not sure, to be honest," Dalton said, looking to Rod. "Our directive is vague."

Rod gave him an understanding nod. "Government work."

Alison looked at him in confusion. "But I don't understand. How can they send you to a foreign country without clear orders? Is that even legal?"

Rod patted her thigh. "Honey, it's the government. You don't question. You do what you're told."

"Okay, but how does that work, then?" Alison asked. "What do you *do*?"

I answered. "We settle into our roles and see what we can ferret out."

Rod seemed satisfied, but Alison wanted to know more. "But what are you even investigating then? You just hang out, see what turns up?"

Rod gave her a let-it-go look.

"It frustrates me, too," I said. "Coincidently, though," I turned to Rod, "I did learn of a mass stranding a few years ago that was caused by Navy sonar. It literally blew some dolphins and whales out of the water. You ever hear anything about that?"

"No," he said, shaking his head. "But I don't know why I would have."

Our waitress approached with our meals and drinks on a large tray. She plopped baskets, brimming with fries, in front of the others, then, as if an afterthought, dropped my salad and bowl of peas and rice in front of me.

"Ketchup's there," she said, pointing at the bottle at the center of the table, and walked away.

Dalton shook a ketchup bottle upside down until a blob hit his plate with a splat. He handed the bottle to Rod, who shook the bottle upside down until a blob hit his plate with a splat. Alison stared at Rod, then back at Dalton, then shook her head.

"How long are you here on the island?" Dalton asked.

"Two weeks. Just got here," Rod answered.

A gull swooped down, snatched a French fry from Alison's basket, causing her to jerk back from the table. It fluttered around the basket, then launched into flight again.

The waitress appeared, shooing with her hands. "Don't feed them birds. Don't do it."

"What?" Alison said. "It just swooped in."

"Don't feed them," the woman repeated and turned her back, annoyed.

We all looked to each other, our eyes flitting around, and burst out laughing.

"So, the post office, huh?" Dalton said.

Rod shrugged. "I worked there before I joined up. They gotta hold the job for veterans, so, I figured it's solid. Good benefits, good retirement."

"Yeah, yeah," Dalton said, nodding as though he agreed that it was a good move.

"Remember the crazy shit we used to do? That nightmare jump?"

Dalton threw back his head and laughed. "Oh God, that was insane. Absolute worst night of my life. Hands down."

"Nightmare jump?" Alison clearly had no idea what they were talking about and I was dying to know what could make Dalton laugh like that. There was a camaraderie between Rod and him that was very different from the partnership we had.

Rod looked at Dalton with barely contained amusement. "Can I tell it, dude? It's probably fine now, right?"

Dalton sat back in his seat. "Be my guest, man. Alison can't get mad at me now and Poppy will probably appreciate it."

"Okay, so we've got a jump mission to a remote area…"

"Where?" Alison had a sparkle in her eye, enjoying seeing her husband telling a story.

Dalton answered. "That's classified, ma'am," he said to her before winking at me.

"Classified. Thank God," Rod laughed, grabbing another fry and stuffing it in his mouth before continuing. "So, it's a tandem night jump, which is fine except we're jumping with civilian interpreters. My dude was totally fine, stuffed him onto my front pack like he was riding in a Babybjorn."

"You lucky bastard." Dalton tipped up his beer and took a swig through his smile.

"Dalton's guy was big as he is, a freaking anomaly for that part of the world, musta walked around his country like a freaking god. So, I've got the hobbit strapped to the front of me and Dalton's got Godzilla and we're getting ready to make the jump and Dalton's monster decides he ain't going."

"Like trying to put a cat in a bathtub," Dalton added.

I can't stop grinning imagining Dalton wrestle with Godzilla.

"We got to our landing zone, so I have to make the jump with my little guy and leave Dalton to deal with crazy."

"I bear hugged him," Dalton said, "and had to hip check him down the loading ramp. He freaked out and sent us into a death spiral. By the time I got that under control, we were cruising under the canopy through some heavy moisture."

"Canopy?" Alison asked.

"The parachute," I said. I knew a little of the lingo.

"Heavy moisture?" Rod was rolling with laughter now.

"We don't have to tell that part," Dalton warned but was

starting to laugh pretty hard himself.

Rod started back up, "We're wearing night vision goggles, so it's hard to tell what's what, really, it all looks like pea soup." Tears are free flowing down his face now.

I had never seen Dalton so animated, so happy. SEAL life really was a different world and he obviously loved it. With his buddy, it was like he was free to be completely himself. "Bad joke, buddy, bad joke."

Alison and I were trying to play catch-up and it must have shown on our faces because Rod explained. "Vomit. Dalton's thinking he's flying through a cloud and picking up heavy moisture and really it's Godzilla unloading his last meal."

"Omigod," I covered my mouth and pushed the remains of my lunch away.

Alison smacked her husband's shoulder with her cloth napkin. "That's not a lunchtime story." But she was clearly amused.

Dalton shrugged and took another sip of his beer. "You don't miss that stuff, buddy?"

"Aww man, I miss the guys, the crazy stories, but it's time for me to settle down, you know, with a kid on the way."

That made Alison grin.

"Yeah," Dalton said. Did I see a little envy in his eyes?

Rod looked at Alison with an expression that no one could mistake. They were happy together. Two people madly in love. Married, with a child on the way.

Was that what Dalton had wanted? After he left the Navy? To settle down? Have a few kids?

Of course he did. Why hadn't I seen it before? He'd married her, hadn't he? *She* was that kind of woman. They'd have had that life together. Regular. Settled. In one place. With a swing set in the backyard.

The shape-shifting anxiety stirred in my stomach again.

My dad had looked at my mom that way. No matter what

came between them, he'd loved her, unconditionally. But a life like that would never have worked for them. And it wouldn't for me either.

"Well, I need to use the ladies room," I said and rose from my chair.

Alison pushed back her chair and rose. "I'll go with you."

I've never understood women who must go to the bathroom in twos, but oh-kay.

We headed down the stairs to the restrooms, which were on the first floor where they were accessible for the pool users as well.

After I'd gone, I waited near the sink for her. That was the thing to do, right? I paced. We were alone. This was my chance to ask her about Dalton. Anything. But what? It felt so…intrusive. *Gee, why would you divorce a guy like Dalton? Or did he divorce you? Just what happened? I know it's none of my business, but spill anyway. I want every gory detail.*

Omigod, I'm losing it.

She came out of the stall and went to the sink to wash her hands. "I hope this isn't too awkward for you, meeting Dalton's ex-wife, and all."

"Not at all. Why would it be?" *Tell me everything.*

She threw the paper towel into the wastebasket and turned to me. "Well, since you're his girlfriend."

I shook my head and backed away. "Oh, no. You got it wrong. I mean, our cover is, but no. We're not—"

She stared at me with skeptical eyes. "All right," she said. But I could tell she didn't believe me. Well, what did it matter anyway?

I turned and walked out of the bathroom. She followed. I came to a halt, turned back to face her. "What makes you think we're together?"

"I can just tell."

I eyed her a moment. *Tell how?* I crossed my arms. *Crap.*

I knew it would be an issue with us, working together, undercover.

I opened my mouth to—was that man following me? He was leaning on a post, smoking a cigarette, his eyes on me. I'd seen him somewhere before. In the crowd. On the beach. Where the dolphin had stranded.

Probably a coincidence. It was a small island.

And yet, the way he'd looked at me, then looked away.

I took Alison by the arm. "We should get back upstairs."

Her eyes grew wide. "Is there something wrong?" She looked around.

"I'm not sure. Let's just get back upstairs."

CHAPTER 6

Kerrie wasn't in the office again. I wanted to poke around, see if I could find anything that might give me a clue, but she'd given me hours of computer work to do.

I called Greg, our analyst and tech support at our Chicago headquarters. Greg was one of those young, nerdy types who could eviscerate an online security system in five point seven seconds. Our first interaction hadn't exactly been a treat.

He answered on one ring. "Yo."

"Yo, yourself."

"What?"

"Nothing. This is Special Agent McVie."

"I know."

"Well, of course you do."

"So, you're in Bimini, Bahamas. How's the weather?"

"Nice—"

"I've got your GPS coordinates."

"Well, that's…comforting."

"Whew. Eighty six degrees and sunny."

"Wow. You've Googled the weather?"

"I do have a degree in computer science."

"Excellent. Speaking of that—"

"So, are you wearing a bikini right now?"

Eye roll. "That's an inappropriate question."

"What I want to know is, how does one get such an

assignment? Sand, sun. Bahama Mama's. I could use a couple
tropical rum drinks on the job. What is it that you've got that
I don't?"

"Do you enjoy getting shot at?"

Pause. "What can I do for you?"

"I want to go through the office here, while the researcher
is gone, see if I can dig up anything, but I have a mountain of
actual intern work to do. It's all computer stuff."

"Uh-huh," he said, clearly anticipating what I was going to
ask next.

"Can you get someone there, one of our interns to do it, so
I can use the time—"

"What are we talking about here?"

"It's easy. Looking at pictures, sorting dorsal fins, that kind
of thing. The files are all in the cloud."

"And how should I log that? Under what billing code? I'm
not familiar with *fin sorting*."

"Are you serious?"

After a long pause, he said, "What's in in for me?"

I sat on the line, silent, giving him the same long pause.

"I'll take care of it."

I gave him the information he needed and disconnected.

Now. I looked around the tiny office, the piles of folders on
the desk, the filing cabinet with one drawer ajar. *Where do I
start?*

Atop the desk was one of those hand-therapy, stress-squeeze
balls, the kind you get free at a convention with some logo
plastered on the side, a mason jar full of sharks' teeth, and a
pencil can stuffed so full of pens and pencils, if you pulled one
out, they'd all come tumbling out with it.

Under the desk was a fifty-year accumulation of dust balls.

The folders turned out to be mostly clerical stuff—some old
intern applications, nonprofit status forms, petty cash requests.
Nothing seemed like a red flag, but I took pictures with my

phone and sent them to Greg as well.

I sat back in the chair. Hanging on the wall behind the desk were several photos of Kerrie, each with a young man or woman, presumably former interns.

My phone rang and I spun toward it with a start.

It was Greg, calling me back.

"Yo," I answered.

"Yo yourself."

"Right. What's up?"

"I've got someone here to plod through these files, but I need you to let me know when you plan to leave the office there, so we can make sure login times match."

"Sure," I said, thankful he was thinking of those details.

When we disconnected, I stared at a photograph on the wall. It was two dolphins, underwater, side by side, suspended in a beautiful stream of sunlight in their surreal monochrome world.

"What's going on with you?" I whispered to the image. "If only you could talk."

A spokesman. The idea popped into my head as if the words came from the image. Ask a spokesman. Someone who knows dolphins better than anyone. *Dr. Parker!*

April Parker, Ph.D., is a biologist who studies killer whale vocalizations. Since killer whales are dolphins, she'd have some insight for me for sure. Dalton and I had met Dr. Parker in Norway when we were there chasing a criminal. She'd been very helpful on the case. I was sure she'd help me if she could.

I searched my phone for her number.

She answered on the fifth ring.

"Agent McVie, how are you?"

"I'm great. You?"

"Good. And Agent Dalton? How is he?"

A twinge of jealousy tightened my stomach. She and Dalton

had an undeniable attraction. In fact, I wasn't sure what exactly had happened between them. *Oh stop! What if something did? He's not my boyfriend. He wasn't then. And he's not now.*

"Good. Good. He's good."

"Is there something I can help you with?"

"Yes. Dolphins. We're on a case, here in Bimini and—"

"Bimini? Has something happened?"

"No. Not exactly. Actually, I don't know. That's what I was hoping you could help me determine."

I told her what I knew—about the Navy incident, the recent stranding of one bottlenose dolphin, Kerrie's claim that all was well.

"From what I've read," she said, "most of the research being done there is with the Atlantic spotted dolphins. The bottlenose dolphins aren't as approachable. And it's a healthy population overall. The Navy took responsibility for that mass stranding incident and claims it was an isolated case."

"I'm at a loss here," I said.

"If my memory serves me," she said, "isn't the research being done there a non-invasive approach? Their data is collected by observation only, right?"

"Yes. Kerrie made that clear on the swim boat. They don't touch the dolphins for anything."

"But you said the stranded bottlenose had a satellite tracker."

I sat back in the chair, my mouth open. *How did I miss that? I can't believe I missed that.*

"The thing is," she said, "bottlenose can be resident or transient. If it was migrating, that could explain it. But…"

"But what?"

"Tell me again about the behavior of the one that approached the boat."

I described the way it bobbed and squealed.

"Yeah, that's not the behavior of a deep water, transient

dolphin."

"What are you saying?"

"Was there anything else unique about that dolphin or the stranded one? Vocalizations? Any scars or distinct marks?"

"Yes, now that you mention it. The stranded one did. Maybe the other, but I didn't see. I mean, they could be the same dolphin. But the stranded one had scars on the base of the flippers. What do you think it means?"

"Well, I have a guess."

"And?"

"It's a long shot guess."

"Your expert guess is better than my fumbling around."

"I think what you've got there is a trained dolphin."

"Trained?" I sat back, stunned. She was right. It was so clear. The way the dolphin came up to the boat, trying to get attention from the humans, begging for a fish. "I think you're right. It makes sense. But trained to do what?"

"I don't know. But the rub marks suggest it has had something strapped to it. Maybe it carried something? A modified backpack?"

"So, someone here is training dolphins to carry something? But what? And who?"

"Can't help you with that. But as far as the dolphin's behavior, that's my best guess, yes. Someone has trained that dolphin."

I looked up at the photo of Kerrie on the wall. *What have you been up to?*

I called an urgent meeting of the team. We agreed that a rendezvous after dark was best.

Meanwhile, I sorted through the remaining folders and found nothing suspicious, nothing that suggested Kerrie had any interest or experience in dolphin training.

When the clock finally rolled over to five, I texted Greg, notifying him I was leaving the office, then locked up and headed out. I grabbed a bite to eat at the snack shack and paced until the sun went down.

Tom and Mike were cleaning the galley after their dinner when I slipped onto the boat. I quickly looked around the salon. "Where's Dalton?"

Tom paused from towel-drying a plate. "Not here yet."

"Right," I said.

"You got something?" Mike asked.

"Yeah, but we should wait for Dalton."

He pulled the plug from the sink and the soapy water sputtered down the drain.

"Beer?"

"Sure."

He grabbed a cold bottle of Sierra Nevada from the refrigerator, popped off the top, and handed it to me.

"We still got nothing," Tom said. "I'm curious to hear what you've found."

"Not nothing," Mike said, admonishing Tom. "We caught three fish and managed to get close to several other boats. This obnoxious fishermen ruse is working out swell. Didn't learn anything, but"—he grinned—"we're eating well."

Dalton came through the door. Mike handed him a beer without asking.

"Thanks, man," Dalton said and sat on the bench on the other side of the boat, a spot where he wasn't right next to me.

"So, what's up?" Tom said sliding into the seat across from me.

I launched into the whole story. When I mentioned April Parker, I kept my eyes on Dalton, but he didn't make the tiniest twitch.

"So that's it. At least one dolphin out there, maybe two, have had significant interactions with humans, possibly even training of some sort, and that training might involve carrying something."

"Any idea what?" Tom asked.

Mike leaned forward. "Drugs, most likely. We're only fifty miles from Miami."

"With the history of Bimini," Dalton said, "that makes the most sense. In the eighties, high-speed Cigarette boats ran cocaine and marijuana from here to Florida every night. Drug smugglers practically took over the island of South Bimini. U.S. patrol boats were chased off with gunfire and the Bahamian military couldn't get control of the situation. DEA finally shut it down."

"But those boats could carry huge cargo," I said. "And like you said, they'd go every night. What can one dolphin carry?"

Tom swallowed a swig of beer, set the bottle on the table. "Enough for one guy to get rich, I would think."

"Or one gal," Dalton said.

"I don't know." I shook my head. "I just don't see it."

"Work on this tiny island isn't exactly lucrative," Mike said. "It's gotta be hard to make ends meet."

That was true. I remembered the Hilton and all the boarded up motels and restaurants. Natalie's family. Could Natalie be involved? No, that didn't feel right either. But my intuition was all out of whack. "Okay, but one person running a tiny parcel of drugs? Do you really think that's what we were sent here to find?"

"Maybe this is a test run. Maybe there are plans to train a whole fleet of dolphins," Mike said.

"Maybe," I said. It didn't set well either.

Dalton spoke up. "Poppy makes a good point though. What popped up on whose radar to get us sent down here? Did DEA request us because of the animal involvement? If so, why weren't we clued in to begin with?"

Tom shook his head. "Dunno."

"Well, you two have worked for Hyland longer than we have," Dalton went on. "Is this common? No intel. No explanation."

"She came on after we were already on the case in Chicago," Mike said. "It makes no sense to me. But I do as I'm told."

Right. Like last time. Mike was the epitome of the rogue agent. For all I knew, he had all kinds of information he wasn't sharing. It wasn't a stretch considering how he handled our last operation. I had forgiven him but I wasn't stupid enough to forget.

"I'm sure there's some point to keeping us in the dark," said Tom. "Maybe if they gave us direction, it would come with bias."

"Maybe," Dalton said, but I could tell he wasn't buying it.

"Well, I don't like it," I said. "We're not children."

"Well, should we call in what we have?" Tom asked.

"Which is what?" Mike said. "A dolphin that may or may not be trained? With marks that may or may not be from carrying something?"

"Or should we wait until you call it in yourself and take the lead?" It popped out of my mouth before I could stop it. Okay, I definitely still didn't trust him.

"Mike's right," Dalton said, giving me a silencing look. "There's no reason to call in yet." He looked to Tom. "The stranding incident must be related." His eyes swung around to me. "Didn't you say that underwater noise could be the cause?"

I nodded.

He turned back to Tom. "Why don't you guys look into the noise issue? Drop your hydrophone in the water. See if you pick up anything interesting. And keep an eye out for anything else. Poppy and I will keep up our charade, poke around to learn some more about these researchers, and see what else comes up."

"Will do," Tom said.

"We'll also check out the nightlife on the island," Mike said. "See if we can pick up some babes."

I held back an eye roll.

"Hey," Mike said, "when you're given a role to play, you need to do it right. One hundred percent. All in, baby."

Tom smirked.

I left the boat, Dalton on my heels.

"Hey," he said, taking my hand. "We've got our roles to play, too. What do you say we head back to your place?"

My insides got all tingly and my head felt light. All it would take was one kiss on my neck and I'd spiral out of control again. I shook my head. "I don't know."

He came to a stop, tugging on my hand, turning me to face him. "Talk to me."

"About what?" As if I didn't know what he meant.

He leaned closer, looked confused. "Are you avoiding me now?"

"No. Why would you say that? It's just that…we have work to do. We can't get distracted."

"Distracted?" He gave me a wicked smile. "It's part of our cover to get under the covers."

"Cute."

The smile faded. "What work do you have to do at nine thirty at night that can't wait until tomorrow?"

"I'm just saying."

He frowned. "You're just saying what?" He stared at me for a long moment. "Is this about Alison?"

"No." I said it too quickly. Sharply.

He stared some more. "Because whatever you want to know, I'll tell you."

"It's not my…I mean…it's not like we…you don't have to—"

He stared at me some more, trying to figure me out.

"It's none of my business."

He looked hurt but I didn't know what else to say. Before he could stop me I turned and left him standing in the streetlight.

He didn't follow and I didn't look back. *Shit*.

I tossed in my bed. Dalton. I didn't want to think about him. I didn't want to think about it. *It*. The thing. Between us.

It was just sex! Geez, why does everyone make such a big deal out of it?

Maybe a sleeping pill would help. The light in the bathroom flickered on when I flipped the switch. I looked into the rusty old mirror. "You look like hell."

I knew it. I knew I shouldn't have had sex with him. I knew it. Now everything was going to be weird. Plus the Alison thing *did* bother me and I *did* want to know what had happened. Why did I say I didn't care?

"And now you've gone and hurt his feelings, Poppy. What the hell is wrong with you?"

The mirror-mirror-on-the-wall told me nothing in return, but the face reflected there looked forlorn.

I can't believe I've screwed this up already.

My toiletry bag held the basics. There had to be some Benadryl or something in there to help me sleep.

I had to get some sleep. I had to be on my game. Focused. I'd already missed too much. Distracted. Not good.

It's just the timing. That's all. Bad timing. That's why I just…I don't know.

I leaned forward, looked into my own eyes. "How did you even know you hurt his feelings? This is Dalton you're talking about. He shows no emotion. Ever."

I closed my eyes. *He wanted me to know.*

Dammit!

Dawn finally came, welcomed, and a hot cup of coffee calmed my head.

No one was in the office when I arrived. I flipped on the window air conditioning to get rid of the stale night air and plopped down in the old, steel swivel chair.

Now what? I needed to swivel my head back on.

I stared at the pictures on the wall. The past interns. All smiles and youthful enthusiasm. Had they liked their job here? Who wouldn't like swimming with dolphins? Sure, I had to do some boring computer work, but, otherwise, it was a dream job. Except maybe working with Kerrie. Though, I had the feeling she was under some kind of stress, and having me forced upon her didn't help. She was probably a joy to work with otherwise. I bet the interns really liked her and—*that's it.* The last intern. He or she might know something.

I found the folder labeled interns and sorted through the paperwork to find the most recent one. Skylar Molton.

I got Greg on the phone to track her down. Within moments he found her current whereabouts. Mississippi. Attending the Gulf Coast Research Laboratory at the University of Southern Mississippi.

"Her thesis is on the impact of underwater sound on dolphin distribution," Greg told me.

Interesting. "I need to talk to her," I said. "Can you find me an obituary?"

"A what?"

Ha. Caught him off guard. "I need a dead grandpa, one I need to fly home to the funeral for. Just for an overnight."

"Oh, right. Gotcha. I'm on it."

Within moments, Greg texted me the details for a funeral service in Brooklyn that matched the last name of my cover name.

I dialed my friend Chris. He's been my best friend since we

were kids. He's a flight attendant and he could get me on a plane faster than the agency. Problem was, I never knew where he was on the planet at any given time and if he'd answer.

While it rang, I grabbed the rubbery ball that sat on the desk and gave it a squeeze.

"Hey girl," Chris chirped. He's the only person in the world who gets to call me girl.

"Hey. I hate to bug you on this, but I'll get right to it. I need to be on a plane to Biloxi, Mississippi tonight. Can you get me on one?"

"Where are you now?"

"Oh yeah, I'm in Bimini, Bahamas."

"What are you doing there?"

"Job. Something's going on with the dolphins. We're not sure what. It's rather vague actually." I switched the ball to the other hand, squeezed a few times.

"So, you're there with Dalton?"

"Yeah."

"What was that?"

"What was what?"

"You hesitated."

"I don't know what you mean."

"I asked about Dalton. You hesitated."

"No I didn't."

He sucked in his breath. "You *didn't?*"

"What?" *Dammit!*

"You *did*." He drew out the word did. "You two finally did the deed. Oh, thank God. I thought I was going to have to get you two drunk and throw you into a hot tub naked together. Soooooooo?"

"So, nothing." I switched the squeeze ball back to the other hand.

"Oh, no. That ain't gonna fly, chicky. Spill. And I mean, *spill*."

My stomach clenched. "There's nothing to spill."

"Don't make me get on a plane and wring it out of you."

"Okay, yeah, so, we had sex. So what? It's not like I'm a virgin or anything. Geez. It was just sex. You don't have to read anything into it."

There was silence. Dead silence.

"You still there?"

"Poppy! What the hell is wrong with you? For months now, it's been Dalton this, Dalton that. What do I do about Dalton? You've been a hot mess with the hots for that hotty Dalton. And now you say it was nothing?"

"Well, it's not like—"

"Okay, listen. This is Chris you're talking to. And I'm not judging. I know what's happened. This whole *development* has scared the pants off you, hasn't it?"

"There's no *development*, it's just, nothing really." The ball got harder to squeeze. "Except…"

"Except what?"

"Well, I'm on this case. And the first day I get here, there's a stranded dolphin. It had a satellite tracker attached to its dorsal fin. Then, when I met the researcher here, who could be a suspect, she told me their studies here are observational only. No physical contact whatsoever. I didn't connect the dots. Someone else had to point that out."

"What the hell are you talking about?"

"The tracker. If they don't touch the dolphins at all, then—"

"What does that have to do with Dalton?"

"Don't you see? My brain is slipping. I'm not paying attention to my job."

"Your *job*? You just finally—and you think because—all right. I know how stubborn you can be. Sure, it's nothing. It was just sex. I can go with that. Like you said, sex doesn't have to mean anything." Another silence. "I'm going to get that Biloxi plane ticket arranged for you."

"Chris, don't be like that."

"Be like what? You said it was no big deal. Then it's no big deal."

"Right. It's no big deal." My hand clamped down hard on the ball.

"Other than it impacted your brain. Your job."

"Right."

"I'll text you the flight numbers."

"Okay."

He hung up.

Dammit! I threw the ball against the door. It made a loud, satisfying bang.

CHAPTER 7

Kerrie didn't care one iota that I had to leave for a funeral. In fact, she seemed relieved.

As Chris had promised, I was on the afternoon flight. Boarding the pontoon ferry, which takes passengers fifty yards across the harbor to the south island, where the commercial airport is, I noticed the man who had been watching me and Alison at the Bimini Big Game Bar & Grill was also on board. He wouldn't make eye contact with me, but when I turned away, I could feel his gaze. Was he following me? My gut told me yes. But I couldn't sort out why he'd be following me, an intern.

After the five minute bus ride, the man quickly disappeared into the building. When I got on the plane, he was already seated, five rows behind me. Maybe I was imagining it. The island is so small, not many commercial flights come and go. Could've been a coincidence. But then, if he was following me, he wouldn't have to stay close. There was only one plane.

In Miami, as I made my way through the customs line, I noticed him again, ahead of me. If I had to keep my eyes on someone in an airport, I'd make sure I was ahead in line, so I could follow immediately once my target got through.

But as I exited the customs area, he was nowhere to be seen.

Hm.

During my two hour layover, I paced an irregular route around the airport, into shops, and back out again. If he was following, it would be hard to keep track of me in the crowd.

On the plane to Biloxi, there he was again. With no carry-on baggage. Just a newspaper rolled up in his hand.

What were the odds he'd be going to Biloxi today as well?

As soon as I got off the plane, I beelined for my cheap rental car and hightailed it out of there. Two miles down the road, I noticed I had a tail. A blue Ford Taurus. I took an off ramp, then, at the light, gunned it straight through. The Taurus followed.

At the next off ramp, I slowed and near the stop light, I pulled off onto the shoulder. As the Taurus went by, I turned to see the driver. It wasn't the man. The Taurus made a right turn and disappeared in traffic.

Okay. What the hell? Was my imagination getting away with me?

I got back on the highway. The Taurus was long gone.

I drove to the campus in Ocean Springs, a fifty-acre peninsula surrounded by water with a tiny research lab, a few dorms, a cafeteria with a nice porch and surprisingly few classrooms. The research vessels, I learned, were docked fourteen miles away in Biloxi.

I hoped Skylar was on campus today, rather than out on one of the boats. Greg had sent her photograph, but was unable to acquire her schedule.

"My god, it's hot here. I'm on my third iced tea," I told Greg on the phone.

"So, you're just sitting around?"

"It's dinner time. I'm at the cafeteria. My best bet. But if there is any other way you can think of to get her schedule—"

"I could ping her phone for you."

"What?" I sat upright. "You can do that?"

"Sure. Hold on."

"Are you serious? Why didn't you tell me—"

"She's crossing the campus now. Heading right for the cafeteria."

"Well, thanks." I hesitated. "Hey, is there any chance you could track a phone without the number?"

"What do you mean?"

"Like, could you find a phone that was on Bimini, then here, now, in Mississippi? In other words, one that followed the same route as mine at the same time?"

"Not retroactively. Not without a subpoena."

"What if my life's in danger?"

"Is it?"

"I think I'm being followed."

"Hm. I can identify the phones being used there now, then cross check that with phones used later on Bimini. Maybe."

"Well, that will have to—holy crap, there he is." The man sat alone at a table across the cafeteria, facing me. "This can't be a coincidence."

"What can't be a coincidence?"

"That he's here. But man, how did he do it?"

"What do you mean?"

"In the airport. How'd he know to get on the plane to Biloxi? And then, I was sure I ditched that Taurus. How'd he find me?"

"Okay, you need to take a breath."

"This can't be a coincidence. I'm being followed by someone with some serious connections. He's a shadow."

"Why do you think—?"

"I need you to triangulate, whatever, do the magic you do, and track him by his phone."

"I'll try. But like I said—"

"Yeah, whatever you can get. Do it."

"Yes ma'am." He disconnected.

And don't ever tell me to take a breath again. Or call me

ma'am.

A young woman walked into the cafeteria who matched Skylar's description—long sandy-brown hair pulled back into a ponytail, a sturdy build, T-shirt and jeans shorts. A Nebraskan farm girl. She was with a young man. Maybe her boyfriend? They moved through the line and chose a table on the porch.

My shadow didn't reveal any recognition of her.

Well, I needed to do what I came here for.

I had the choice of several approaches: tell her I wanted to try for an internship and ask her advice about her experience, tell her I was doing a follow-up survey on her experience there, or the straight truth, that I'm a federal agent and needed honest information. I decided I'd know which tack to take when I met her.

I moved from my spot, went right to her table, and pulled out an empty chair beside her where I still had a good view of my shadow.

"Hi, it's Skylar, right?"

"Yeah," she nodded. "Have we met?"

"No. I've been hoping to meet you, though."

She seemed confused by this, but kindly gestured toward her friend. "This is JP."

He nodded.

"Nice to meet you. What does JP stand for?" I asked.

He grinned. "I could tell you, but I'd have to kill you."

"Ah, cute." Flirting with me. Okay, not her boyfriend.

I turned back to Skylar. "I was hoping I could ask you some questions."

Her cheeks turned rosy. "Gosh, you sound like a cop."

"Actually—" I pulled my badge from my purse and held it under the table where only she could see it. "I am. I'm a federal agent."

JP leaned over her to see the badge and gulped.

Skylar's eyes grew large. "Is there something wrong?

What's happened?"

"Well, that's what I'm here to find out."

"Have I done something?" Her voice had a hint of panic.

"No, no." Maybe that wasn't the right approach. "No worries. I just think you might have some information that can help me on a case."

"I don't know how I can help, I mean, with whatever it is you need help with, but, sure, whatever. Ask away."

"Why don't you start by telling me about your thesis project."

She cocked her head to the side, genuinely taken aback. "I'm studying the impact of underwater sound on dolphins. Nothing illegal. Just...unfortunate. I mean, I wish it were illegal, but..."

"Is that what you were working on during your internship in Bimini?"

"No, not then. But I was inspired by the noise generated by the building of the pier there over the last few years." She looked at me more shrewdly. "The research team already has a ton of data that I can catalog, instead of having to collect new data."

"And what have you found?"

"Nothing yet, I'm still working on the funding. I did get approval to go ahead with it though. But you know, time is money. So it's barely started. I'm not sure I'd have any information to help you."

"All right. I have a few other questions, okay?"

She shifted in her chair. "Okay."

JP held his fountain Coca-cola cup with two hands and chewed on the straw.

I glanced at the man. Still there.

"So, you must be aware of the mass stranding a few years ago, the one caused by the Navy," I said.

"Yeah," Skylar said with an exaggerated nod. "Everybody

knows about that. It was a big deal because the Navy actually took responsibility. Like, formally took responsibility."

"You mean that it was their sonar that caused the problem? The sound?"

"In that case, yes. Sonar is devastating to whales and dolphins. The Navy is basically pushing extremely loud waves of sound across wide swathes of the ocean. Whales react in the same way they would in the presence of an enormous predator. They go silent, stop foraging, and abandon their habitat. Worse, the sound can actually burst their eardrums and cause hemorrhaging in their brains. Military sonar has caused mass strandings all over the world. It's not a mystery. The whales are trying to get the hell away from it.

"But it's not just Navy sonar that's a problem. The ocean is getting more and more noisy everyday. Commercial vessels create a cacophony of noise. The cavitation from their propellers sounds like gunshots to a whale. And their engines make a perpetual rumble. Then there's the industrial noise. The oil and gas industry uses seismic airguns, the modern form of exploratory dynamite, that discharge extremely intense pulses of sound toward the sea floor. During seismic surveys, acoustic explosions can continue for days or weeks on end. Reports say things like"—she held up fingers and made quotes in the air —"'The blasts disrupt critical behavior and communication among whales.' But my god, can you imagine? These whales, in their lifetime, have gone from a silent world, where they could call out, 'Hey Bob,' for miles and miles away, to not being able to hear their own voice amid the unbearable, incessant noise."

She was obviously very passionate about this issue. I said, "I imagine with commercial, industrial, and even military activity, there are a lot of people who don't want to see any science about the problems all the noise is causing. Are you concerned about pushback or even threats?"

"Me personally? No. I mean, it's just a study. It's not in-your-face like the Sea Shepherds or something."

"What do you know about training dolphins?"

Skylar crossed her arms. "Other than I don't agree with it?"

JP slurped the last of his Coca-cola, but held the straw between his teeth as he said, "Especially the part where they're captured and kept captive, for sure."

"Have you ever heard of anyone training dolphins outside a captive facility? Like dolphins in the wild?"

Skylar shook her head. "No. And I don't see how that'd be feasible. I mean, dolphins are usually trained with operant conditioning. You'd have to find a pretty significant reward system."

"What's operant conditioning?" I asked. I thought I knew, but hearing a scientist's explanation would be helpful.

"In general, it's where rewards and punishments are used to change or encourage certain behavior. You've heard of Pavlov's dogs, right? It's similar. For example, when a lab rat presses a lever, he receives a food pellet as a reward, but when he presses a button he receives a mild electric shock. As a result, he learns to press the lever but avoid the button. But that's in a controlled environment. For one, negative reinforcement is not used on dolphins. At least not in the United States. And I can't think of any reward that would lure wild dolphins for any conditioning to happen."

"Actually," JP chimed in, "there was an event during Hurricane Katrina. Well, kinda."

I turned to him. "What do you mean?"

"Some of the bottlenose dolphins that were captive at Marine Life Oceanarium in Gulfport were washed out of the pool and into the Mississippi during the storm surge. It was twelve days before the trainers could go out and look for them. They were spotted together, just outside Gulfport Harbor. The trainers called the dolphins to the rescue boat with whistle blasts, typical recall protocol. They were fed and checked out by the medics. But there was a problem."

Skylar nodded in agreement. "Getting them back into the oceanarium."

"Right," JP said. He seemed pleased to be able to contribute to the conversation.

"So, what'd they do?" I asked.

"They had to work on some new training out there in the Gulf. Basically, they set up floating mats and trained them to haul out onto the mats where they could then be wrapped in slings for transport. It was actually a significant research event. We learned a lot from that one unplanned situation."

"Like what?" I asked.

"Well, dolphins have a fission-fusion society. That means individuals interact in small groups that change often, but they maintain relationships within the larger community. We already knew that. What we learned from the Katrina event, was that the dolphins who had been captive together, stayed together in the wild. The younger ones followed the lead of the older, more experienced ones. So, the trainers were very careful in the order in which they called them in."

"You seem to know a lot about dolphin training," I said.

He looked down at this hands. "Yeah, well, when I was a kid, I wanted to be a dolphin trainer. You know, at SeaWorld. But then I learned the dark side of it all."

"The dark side?" I knew all about it, but I wanted to hear his take on it.

"You know *The Cove*? How, in Japan, they capture and slaughter dolphins in the wild and choose the healthiest to sell into captivity. It's big business. Lots of money. Now, that's a powerful industry, that's for sure. Is that why you're here?"

I didn't acknowledge the question. "So, in the Hurricane Katrina incident, the dolphins involved had already been trained. But let's say someone found a way to reward, as you say, some wild dolphins in a way that they were able to train them in the wild. What would that look like?"

JP shrugged. Skylar shrugged. JP spoke. "They'd definitely be working from a boat, I would think. Deep water. Not from shore. Unless they set up a floating platform or something. And, I don't know. No, it would have to be a boat, because their territory is so large, calling them in wouldn't really work. Whatever, it would take time. A lot more time than if they were captive." He shrugged again. "I just can't see it. Dolphins are too smart."

"Is there any way to figure out, from interaction with the dolphins, what they're being trained to do?"

They both thought about it, shaking their heads.

At the table across the room, the man set his newspaper on the table, but made no move to go.

"Are you working on a research project, JP?"

"Yes, the impact of the Deepwater Horizon oil spill on reproduction rates in bottlenose dolphins."

"Ah," I said. "I assume not good."

He shook his head. "Not good. The dolphins that died soon afterward had adrenal hormone abnormalities, lesions on their lungs, severe weight loss, primary bacterial pneumonia, among other things. Now, even years later, the ones that survived still suffer from the same ailments. But a significant factor that people don't consider is that many of the dolphins that died were reproductive-aged adults. The lifelong social bonds these dolphins have was severely impacted. Since they're slow to mature and reproduce, it takes the population a long time to recover. Decades. The loss of those adults has had rippling effects on behavior and mating success."

Skylar glanced at her watch.

With a quick glance at my shadow, who was now talking on a cell phone—yes!—I said, "I just have one more question.

When you were on Bimini, did you notice anything out of the ordinary about the dolphins there? Anything unexpected?"

"Do you mean other than the five tagged bottlenose dolphins that showed up?"

I tried not to show any surprise. "Let's start with that."

"Literally, one day, we spotted these five dolphins. Kerrie had never seen them before. They came right up to the boat. Very odd behavior for bottlenose."

"How so?"

"Well,"—an expression of realization came over her, as if her experience and my questions came together—"like they'd been trained."

"How did Kerrie react?"

"She was surprised. Didn't know what to make of it. There was no discernible marking on the tags. When we got back to the office, she tried for days to track down the researchers who'd tagged them. It was a dead end."

"So, she gave up trying to find out?"

"Don't know. I left. My internship was over."

"Do you think it's possible she wasn't surprised at all? That she had been somehow involved in training them?"

"Kerrie? No way. She's as passionate an advocate as I've ever met. If she caught someone even trying to touch a dolphin, she'd read 'em the riot act. No way."

"One of those dolphins got stranded two days ago."

She asked where exactly, what happened. I tried my best to explain the details of the situation.

"Makes sense, I guess," she said, "for a dolphin who doesn't know the area. The resident dolphins wouldn't go up in that shallow bay at low tide."

"So, they are trained dolphins, but from somewhere else?"

Skylar shrugged.

JP nodded in the affirmative. "Makes the most sense."

"Well, thank you. I need you to keep our visit to yourselves.

Don't tell anyone I was here. Okay?"

They nodded.

I glanced over at my shadow, then stared at JP for a moment, making a decision. "JP," I said. "You seem like a good guy."

He hesitated. "Um, yeah?"

"I'm going to be honest. I'm not sure what's going on, exactly. Not yet. But until I do, will you stick with Skylar? Walk her to class, whatever?" I turned to her. "I don't want you out alone. Something's going on and I can't promise you're not in danger."

"Are you serious? I mean, our schedules—"

"Just be cautious. Okay?"

She hesitated, then nodded.

"I promise," JP said, and I felt a little better.

The minutes clicked by as I stayed in my seat, watching what the man would do when Skylar and JP left.

If he wanted to know what I'd come here for, he had his answer. Would he leave? Follow them now? Or continue to follow me?

Back on his phone, he finally made eye contact with me. Then he disconnected, got up, and left the cafeteria in the opposite direction Skylar had gone.

He'd followed me here. I knew he did. I felt it in my bones.

Well, two could play that game.

I got up, moved across the room, and went out the door after him.

He crossed the campus, heading toward a forested area, never looking back. He walked with a slight limp, but seemed to be able to move at a good pace.

Once he entered the woods, he started across a pedestrian suspension bridge that spanned a wooded gully. It was about five feet wide and made of galvanized steel. I hesitated. The bridge was at least 250 feet across. If I started after him and he turned, or stopped, I had nowhere to go. If I waited, I might lose him on the other side.

I stepped onto the bridge. Leafy branches poked through the wire cables. It reminded me of the many suspension bridges in Costa Rica, built to allow a view from the different levels of the rainforest.

As I approached the center of the bridge, it swayed beneath my feet. The man continued on. As he left the bridge, he turned to the left. I hurried across after him.

Once I arrived on the other side, I looked left. A few hundreds yards away was a parking area. But where had he gone? There was no one. I continued on, scanning.

Was his car in the parking lot? Another Ford Taurus?

No car started. No movement.

He'd disappeared.

As I headed back toward the cafeteria and my car, I punched in Greg's number.

"Yo."

"Yo. Why do you answer that way, anyway?"

"Dunno. Why do you repeat it?"

"Dunno. Anything with the phone tracking?"

"Has he gone back to Bimini yet?"

"No."

"Then no."

"Okay. Can you do a search for me, online?"

"What? Don't tell me you don't know how to use Google?"

"Yes, but Google is for amateurs. I need the real thing. A deep search. A search that takes a genius, the kind that—"

"Yep, flattery will get you there every time."

"Great. Consider yourself all buttered up."

"Ah, the visual on that is—"

"I need to know if any trained dolphins have recently escaped their seaside pens. Anywhere in the world."

"Okay."

"So, how long will it take?"

"There are no reports of any trained dolphins having recently escaped their seaside pens."

"How did you—?"

"I Googled it."

"Are you serious?"

"Yep. Anything else?"

I hung up. I had one more call to make.

Dalton answered on the first ring. "Where are you?"

"In Mississippi following a lead. I'll fill you in on that when I get back tomorrow, but right now I need to tell you something else." My tone told him this was business.

"Shoot."

"The other day at lunch, when Alison and I went to the bathroom, there was a man, watching us when we came out. It was unnerving. He seemed familiar to me. Then I realized I'd seen him in the crowd where the dolphin had been stranded."

"What do you mean, watching?"

"Watching. You know, you can feel it. His eyes on you. And the way he looked away when I saw him."

"Why didn't you mention this before?"

"He didn't do anything. It's a small island. The most likely explanation was a simple coincidence."

"But?"

"But then when I went to the airport, he was on the same plane."

"Okay," he said, clearly concerned now.

"Not just to Miami, but on the second flight to Mississippi. That was too much of a coincidence, so I paid very close attention. I swear, there's no way he could have tailed me to the campus. I pulled a couple maneuvers in the car. But then, there he was. In the cafeteria while I was talking with Skylar, Kerrie's last intern."

"And you're sure it was the same man?"

I paused, annoyed.

"All right." He thought a moment. "You're right. That's too big of a coincidence." He thought some more. "And you're sure he didn't follow on the highway."

I shook my head. "No way."

"There are other marine studies going on here in Bimini. And those scientists could be consulting with someone at the research laboratory there. It's not that far-fetched."

"I know."

"But you don't think so."

I paused, thinking. It didn't feel right. He'd been following me. My gut said so. But maybe I was wrong. "No, but I don't know."

"Let me see what else I can dig up over here. In the meantime, be careful. Be safe. Do not take any risks. I'm serious, Poppy."

With no sign of my stalker, I made my early morning flight on time, got settled into my seat, closed my eyes. Maybe I had imagined the whole thing. He wasn't on the plane back to Bimini this morning. Did that mean he wasn't really following me? Or he'd already discovered what I'd come to Mississippi for and didn't feel the need to continue the surveillance.

The seat next to me was empty, so maybe he'd show up yet. I stood up and scanned the aircraft. It was the only remaining seat available. The thought of him ending up right next to me made me grin.

I laid my head back and closed my eyes again.

Why would he follow me, an intern? Had he been watching Kerrie and Natalie too? If so, they probably wouldn't have noticed. Not if he was a pro, which he definitely was.

This whole situation didn't make any sense. Someone was training dolphins. In the wild. Quite possibly—no probably— illegally. Yet in a very visible, highly visited area. And with dolphin researchers—people educated in the behavior of dolphins—living right there. Either Kerrie and Natalie were somehow involved, or the people who were doing it were taking a big risk that they'd be discovered.

But why? What for? What were the dolphins being trained to do? If I could figure that out, I could narrow down the suspects. JP and Skylar had no ideas on how to determine what they'd been trained to do. I needed to figure it out on my own.

The pilots were running through the systems check—lights turned on and off, engines rumbled, mechanical things clanked. Someone plopped down in the seat next to me with such presence that I opened my eyes.

Chris!

"Omigosh," I said. I didn't know whether to be thrilled or annoyed. The expression on his face made my decision. Annoyed.

"All right," he said. "Enough of this denial-avoidance-clammed-up-edness. You're going to talk. I didn't fly across the country to get the it's-no-big-deal speech."

"Are you kidding? What? You've taken time off for this?"

"Yep. Until you talk."

"That's not even funny."

"You don't have to tell me. But if you don't spill by Tuesday, I could lose my job."

Oh, why does this have to be such a big deal? I shifted in my seat. "It's not like we're kids and it's all about the kiss and tell. Geez."

"Okay, dear. That's not what I'm talking about and you know it." He crossed his arms. "Though, I admit, I could use some juicy details. It's been a long dry spell."

Eye roll.

His expression turned to a look of concern. "Seriously. I'm worried about you."

"Seriously, I'm fine."

"We'll see." He pulled a handful of peach-colored yarn attached to a half-finished knitting project from his bag, took hold of the needles, and started to knit.

"Since when did you take up knitting?" I asked.

"I'm knitting knockers."

"You're what? What's a knocker?"

"You know, knockers." He wiggled his finger, pointing at my breasts. "One of my co-workers has breast cancer and the other flight attendants started making them, so I thought, why not? They're for women who've had mastectomies."

"Really? I've never heard of them."

"Yeah. Traditional breast prosthetics are expensive, and heavy, sweaty and uncomfortable. At least, that's what I'm told. And you need a special bra with pockets for them. Knitted knockers on the other hand are soft and comfortable and you can stuff 'em in a regular bra. They look and feel just like real breasts."

He held the knocker for me to give it a squeeze. It even had a nipple knitted in the right place.

"My friend is having reconstruction surgery, so I'm making one that can be altered as she needs by removing some of the stuffing."

I stared at him. My best friend. And this was why. He was sweet, caring, and would do anything for me or anyone in need. I wrapped my arms around him and kissed him on the cheek. "Thanks for coming," I said.

"Anytime," he said with that sassy grin, and the needles went click, click, click.

CHAPTER 8

Dalton was waiting when I got off the ferry. I wasn't expecting him to meet me and was suddenly nervous. We hadn't discussed the conversation, or non-conversation about his ex-wife, and seeing him reminded me of how I'd fled that conversation like an idiot.

"Hey," he said, approaching. "We need to—" He saw Chris behind me. "What's he doing here?" He frowned. "Sorry, Chris. Nothing personal."

Chris winked.

"We're not exactly on vacation here," Dalton said with tense lips.

"He helped me get the flight," I said, as if that explained his presence.

"I'll be at the Hilton," Chris said, then gave me a quick peck on the cheek.

I spun on him. "What? Ugh, not that place."

He shrugged it off. "I've got seven billion points to redeem." He nodded toward Dalton. "Nice to see you again." And he disappeared with the others looking for a taxi.

"You didn't have to meet me at the ferry," I said.

"Tom and Mike have something."

"Oh." It was business.

"They're anchored out in the bay, near the mangroves. We're going to kayak out there."

"Okay," I said. "Let me drop my bag and change my clothes."

We walked to my room, saying nothing more, stuck in an uncomfortable silence. At the door, I said I'd be right out and went inside and shut the door behind me.

Deep breath. *I can handle Dalton. I can roll with it. No problem. Nothing's changed.*

Back at the mirror, I paused for a moment. "Just don't let him in here. He'll have you back in bed before you can say what-about-dinner?"

I lathered on some sunscreen, changed into white capri pants and a short-sleeved, cotton top with a palm frond pattern, grabbed my hat, and I was back out the door.

Dalton was leaning on the wall, his arms crossed, one foot lazily tipped across the other. Reminded me of a cowboy, leaning on a fence, posing for some Cowboy-of-the-Month calendar. I bit my lip and tried to keep my breathing under control. *God, he's hot.*

"Didn't want me to come in your room, huh?" he said, arms still crossed, making no attempt to move.

"I was changing."

"Yeah." His shoulders raised in a little shrug, but his eyes locked onto mine and he lowered his voice. "I've seen you naked."

"So?" I tried to shrug casually. Was I blushing? *Dammit!* I was blushing. "Doesn't entitle you to an all-access pass."

"Uh-huh." He eased away from the wall. "Let's go."

In a two-man kayak from the dive shop—me in the front, Dalton in the back—we pushed off, heading across the bay.

"Let's be careful now," Dalton said. "No fooling around."

"Fooling around?" I glanced back at him. "What are you talking about?"

"In the kayak. Keep it steady and upright. There are a lot of sharks in the bay."

I turned around to see his face. "Are you afraid of sharks?"

"Turn back around and don't rock the kayak."

I giggled. "Omigod, you're afraid of sharks."

"I'm not afraid of sharks. It's the—"

"Ha! Garrett Dalton is afraid of sharks."

"Don't call me that." His voice had lowered an octave.

I started to turn to apologize.

"What'd I say?"

I spun back around to face forward.

"All right, all right. Sorry." Another giggle escaped. "I just didn't know that you're afraid of sharks."

"I'm not. If you'd let me get a word in."

"Okay, go ahead."

"Didn't you know that this is a shark sanctuary?"

"Well, yeah. All of The Bahamas. Since 2011, wasn't it? They prohibit all shark fishing." I spun around. "But sharks aren't—"

"Will you stop?"

"Sorry." I slowly turned back to face forward again.

"Let me finish. Bimini is home to some of the best shark diving in the world. Lemon sharks, nurse sharks, tiger sharks, blacktips, Caribbean reef sharks, bull sharks and occasionally, depending on the season, great hammerheads."

I craned my neck around to look at him. "Yeah, but there's no reason to fear—"

"I swear to God, Poppy, if you don't sit still facing forward I'll knock you unconscious with this paddle."

I shrank. Geez, he was touchy.

"There are a lot of sharks that hang out right here, around the pier, because the fishermen toss all the fish guts in the water right over there." He pointed with the paddle. "So many that the dive shop has capitalized on it. They have a shark cage."

"Oh!" I froze, facing forward.

"So now you get my point."

I nodded, eyes forward. "Feeding sharks. Not good."

"Right."

"Now let's go."

I dipped my paddle in the water and he matched my stroke.

"You know, I kinda like the symbolism."

"Symbolism?"

"Yeah, instead of putting the sharks in a cage, they live free while the people are in the cage. Ha!"

"You would," he said.

I knew he was grinning, but I didn't dare turn around to look.

About halfway across the bay, I glanced over my shoulder, looking back for any sign of being followed.

"Paranoid now?" Dalton asked. "You won't see the sharks."

"I'm just...I'm just checking. You know, make sure no one is following us."

"You're still worried."

"Yeah, well—" I glanced back again, scanned the shoreline. "Maybe," I said, and dug my paddle in, heading for the backside of one of the mangrove-covered islands. The coastal bush-like trees rose from the edge of the water, a wall of green. Perfect cover.

A great egret squawked as it launched from a branch, its huge white wings laboring to keep it airborne.

"Poppy, I've been thinking about it. And what you described, being able to get on a plane like that, last minute, to track you electronically, in real time, would take a level of sophistication that, well, would equal that of the Pentagon. You're talking about hacking airline data, phones."

"You're right. I'm being paranoid." My faced flushed with

embarrassment. I raised my paddle and dug into the water. "Let's get going."

"I'm not saying we shouldn't watch our backs."

"I know." I paddled harder.

Dalton finally dipped his paddle in and we continued past another island to rendezvous with our teammates on their fishing boat.

The scent of frying bacon wafted from the stern. Tom stood at the grill adorned with an apron that said, 'Caught not Bought' with an overlay of a fish skeleton. He turned the bacon with tongs and, with each flip, tiny flames shot up from the grill in a sizzling whoosh.

"I'm not sure it's a good idea to grill bacon," Dalton said. "Too much grease."

"Nah," Tom said, waving it off. "It's thick cut."

Mike helped us tie off the kayak and get out. "I've got pancake batter ready to go. How many will you have?"

"It's, like, noon," I said.

Dalton shook his head. "None for me."

Pancakes sounded good, but I declined. I was too anxious about the case. "What'd you guys find?"

"Oh, I'll make a couple for you," Mike said. "Gotta fuel up. Going to be a long night."

He headed into the galley. I turned to Tom. "What's that mean?"

"We'll lay it all out in a sec." He flipped another hunk of bacon and the flames shot up from the grill.

"Well, on my little jaunt, I learned more about dolphins in general. Nothing earth shattering." I filled them in on my conversation with Skylar and JP while Mike handed Dalton a bottle of syrup and butter to place on the table on the back deck. I left out my suspicions of the potential stalker. Dalton knew and I didn't want them to think I was paranoid, too. "The main point that the students agreed on is that these are trained dolphins, but likely from somewhere else. I did a search online to see if any trained dolphins have escaped their seaside pens, but found nothing."

Tom plucked strips of bacon from the grill, dropping them on a plate covered with paper towel.

Mike emerged with a stack of pancakes and four plates. "Let's eat."

They were irresistible, thick and fluffy. I'd forgotten that Mike was an excellent cook, a redeeming quality. I took two and drizzled a tiny line of maple syrup on top, then cut off a piece with my fork. Ooooh, was it good.

Tom crammed a big, chewy piece of bacon into his mouth and started with the story. "So, we went out fishing last night, after dark and anchored kinda close to this other boat. *Gaspar's Revenge*. The sea was calm as ice. And when it's like that, you know how you can hear people talking, sometimes across the water, like they're right next to you? Well, we could hear these guys talking about a meet, out on the water. Coulda been fishing talk, but sounded a lot like something else." He finally swallowed. "Mike gets the idea to get the hydrophone on and we pointed it in their direction. Seems these guys are making a run to the mainland tonight."

"Drugs?" Dalton asked.

"Didn't say," Mike said, cutting his pancakes with the side of his fork. "But I doubt they were talking about fish. They discussed a port and backup landing location. No one needs a backup for anything legal."

"Right," Dalton said. "You get a time?"

"After dark."

"What do you want to do?"

Tom held another piece of bacon in front of his mouth. "I think we should follow them. Once in U.S. waters, we pull 'em over. Board 'em. See what they've got." In went the bacon.

"Simple plan, I guess," Dalton said, thinking. "What kind of vessel do they have? Is it fast? One of those Cigarette boats?"

"No. Fishing boat, like this one, only newer and faster. All tricked out."

"I looked it up," Mike said. "It's a Rampage. Tops out at forty point three miles per hour. But I figure he won't go full speed. Why waste the gas?"

Dalton thought for a moment. "Engines can be modified. We can't assume from standard specs."

Mike nodded.

"And how do you plan to follow them? Without them knowing?"

"We got radar," Mike said.

"Okay, but we don't have jurisdiction until they're within twelve miles of shore and—"

"I thought we did for this type of thing."

"The Coast Guard does, under an agreement with The Bahamas. But we're not Coast Guard. And I'm not sure we want to blow our cover for this."

Mike shrugged, agreeing.

"You'll need to follow from a distance so you're not obvious. The radar probably has a range of about twenty miles, so that's the max. But then you'll have to cover that distance plus overcome their speed within that twelve miles."

Mike thought about this.

"We'd need a faster boat," Dalton said before Mike had time to put it together. "Following isn't an option. We'll have to coordinate. I could probably take the Zodiac from the dive shop fleet. We could tow it over and Poppy and I could wait inside territorial waters. Then, once they cross the line, we could close the distance much faster."

Mike was nodding, agreeing.

"You'll need to drop us, then backtrack and wait halfway, watching him on your radar. One of you will have to stay back and give the alert when the boat leaves the bay."

Mike looked to Tom. Tom shrugged. "I'll stay back," Mike said.

"In fact, Ron's got a fishing boat—"

"Ron?"

"Captain Ron. Owns the dive shop. He's got a fishing boat docked down at the next marina. He's working on the engine, but I bet he's got radar. You could fire it up to get a fix on our guy as he leaves. I'll talk to him."

Mike and Tom nodded.

"All right," Dalton said. "We need to get on it. All the setup is going to take some time. Let's work out the details. You got a chart?"

Mike shook his head. "Better. I got a RayMarine chartplotter." He fired up the navigation instruments and tapped the screen of the chart plotter. "We're fifty-ish miles from Florida. They could be headed to Miami, Fort Lauderdale, anywhere in between or one side or the other."

"Wherever," Dalton said, "The key will be making sure we're tracking the right boat on the radar from the beginning. There's only one way they'll leave this harbor. Tom, you'll have to make sure you're back within twenty-five miles at least, close enough to pick him up for sure once he's gotten to the outer limits of Mike's range. Then move with him, no more than ten miles ahead, always keeping him on the screen."

Tom nodded.

"Mike, as soon as you get a trajectory, though, send us their probable destination," Dalton went on. "Poppy and I'll head that way in the Zodiac. Tom, you can let him pass you. We'll need you to stay on them on radar and communicate their whereabouts, particularly when they've breached the border, while we try to acquire visual contact. Using the marina radio is too risky. We're going to need secure communication."

"That's a problem," Tom said. "We didn't bring sat phones."

"Yeah, it's fifty miles," I said. "I bet our regular cell phones won't work."

"Hopefully near shore. We don't have any other option, really," Dalton said, snatching the last piece of bacon from the plate. "Unless you brought some sort of tracking device?"

Tom shook his head.

"What if they resist?" I asked. "They could turn right around and head back to Bimini. And then they've seen us. I mean, who says they'll pull over for us? Maybe they'll flip us the bird and keep going."

Dalton crossed his arms, sat back. "Yeah, trying to board them isn't a feasible option. We'll have to follow them into port. Wait until they're tied off or otherwise contained."

"So, you think these are the ones training the dolphins?" I asked.

"Not sure, exactly. But the one said something about getting the mules ready."

"And you think they mean dolphins?"

Tom and Mike both shrugged. Tom said, "By the tenor of the conversation, it seemed like that was a future plan, that they wouldn't have to make these runs for long."

"I guess that fits," I said. "And Skylar and JP seemed to think that if someone was training dolphins in the wild, it would have to be from a boat. Makes sense."

I could feel the energy. We had something. But I still wanted to check it out for myself, get a closer look.

While Dalton went to discuss borrowing the Zodiac from the dive shop, I donned my sunglasses and floppy sun hat and wandered down the road, my eye on *Gaspar's Revenge* anchored in the bay. There was no dinghy tied to the stern. Perhaps the men were ashore right now.

I walked along the stretch of beach near Bailey Town, the closest place to make landfall from the boat, looking for a dinghy pulled up on shore or tied to a dock.

What I did come across, was a pile of conch shells at the water's edge that must have numbered in the tens of thousands. It was right next to Joe's Conch Shack, an open-air grill covered by a dilapidated roof and decorated with years of tourists' graffiti. The place was surrounded by tourists in flip flops holding styrofoam bowls in their hands as they stood, scarfing down conch salad with plastic forks. From the size of the crowd, this was definitely a popular spot.

Eighties music blared from a dented speaker of the same era.

I sat down on the edge of a picnic table and looked toward the boat. It was too far away for me to see what may be happening onboard. Were we really on to something? It didn't feel right.

In the water, something moved. Was it a dolphin? There it was again. If only I had my binoculars. I kept an eye on the moving object as it came closer. It was a man, swimming to shore. He'd come from *Gaspar's Revenge.*

Once in shallow water, he stood and waded toward shore, running a hand through his hair to push off the excess water. September. Of the Cowboy-of-the-Month calendar. Oh yes. He could definitely be September.

No way a drug runner looks like that. Drug runners look like…well, not that.

I caught myself staring.

This man was ruggedly handsome. Probably about six-foot-three and an extremely fit two hundred, twenty-five pounds. His sandy-brown hair was streaked by salt air and sun with a little gray around his ears and on his chin. I guessed he was around fifty years old.

If he hadn't wanted to make a grand entrance, he'd failed miserably. Every woman within a two-hundred yard radius had eyes on him.

He looked over the crowd the way Dalton would—with razor-sharp acuity disguised as a casual glance—and moved toward the shack, digging a few soggy dollars from the pocket of his blue swimming trunks.

I rose from the picnic table, took my hat off and pushed my sunglasses on top of my head as I moved to get in line behind him.

Sliding up close, I could see an ugly scar on his back and another on the top of his left shoulder, both stark white compared to the rest of his tanned body. On his right forearm, he had a tattoo. It was a skull with an old-style scuba regulator in its mouth and crossed oars and wings behind it. It looked military. I made a mental note to ask Dalton about it.

If it was military, he'd seen some action. Explained the way he had assessed the landscape. Yet, somehow he exuded a warm presence, almost zen-like.

"Got your famous Scorch conch today?" he asked, dripping on the sand.

The man at the grill—Joe, I assumed—simply nodded with a smile and served up a bowl.

"And a Kalik," he added as a young girl in braids took his cash.

I leaned on the wooden bar beside him. "What's the Scorch conch? It looks good."

The man turned to answer me and stalled, his eyes quickly traveling down to my knees, then back up to meet mine.

Dude, you're good looking, but you could be my dad. I gave him my best coy smile.

"It's hot," he said with a raise of his eyebrows. "Really hot."

"How hot?" I said, teasing. *Oh geez.*

He seemed to gain control of himself, taking his change from the girl and stuffing it into his pocket. "Joe here makes the hot sauce himself, with locally grown goat peppers. Believe me, it'll knock your socks off. But try it at your own risk. It packs some serious heat."

I grinned. "I think I can handle it."

That made him smile. *Setting the hook.*

I turned to Joe. "And a Kalik as well."

The man dug some more money from his shorts. "Let me get that."

"No need," I said. *Gotcha.*

"It would be my pleasure," he replied. "If you'd care to join me?" He gestured toward a picnic table.

I hesitated, then nodded.

"I'm Jesse," he said.

"Poppy," I replied, waiting for the usual response. But he showed no opinion, one way or another. *Hm. Okay.*

Joe plopped a second bowl in front of us. Jesse tucked his beer under his arm and picked up both bowls. "After you."

I turned toward the tables. *Crap.* I don't eat conch. Any seafood. How was I going to handle this now?

The young girl nudged me with a cold bottle of beer.

I took it from her with a thanks, then led Jesse through the crowd to a table with one end vacant. We sat across from each other.

"So, Poppy,"—he said my name as though he were trying to be respectful—"what brings you to this tiny island paradise?"

I took a sip of my beer, trying to work up the nerve to swallow a piece of a giant snail. "I'm a marine biology intern. I'm an ornithology major, but I got rotated into an internship here."

The corner of his mouth lifted into a grin. "An ornithologist, huh? I can honestly say I've never met one."

"Yep, I'm working on my first million. I figure by the time I'm forty, I'll be set for life."

His eyes lit with amusement. "Well, aren't you a breath of fresh air?"

I shrugged and leaned forward, feigning a whisper. "I'm really just here for the sun and beer."

He laughed. "You can't be serious? Kalik?"

He had a nice laugh. "Ah, there's something about the magic that comes with the sun and the waves and palm trees swaying in the wind. An ice cold, watered-down excuse for a beer can really hit the spot."

He let loose a whole-hearted chuckle. The others at the table paused and turned to look our way. We looked at each other and laughed again.

"So, what brings *you* to this tiny island paradise?" I asked. *Besides ogling young hard bodies in bikinis.*

"Nothing," he said, without a moment's hesitation. "I'm a lost soul, wandering the ocean blue, looking for meaning in it all."

"And have you found any?" *Besides running drugs? If that's what you're doing.*

"Nah." He held up his bottle of Kalik, examined the contents. "I think it's the beer. A stronger brew would help with the clarity, though. Kinda like peyote and a vision quest." He nodded, satisfied with his analogy. "Yeah, maybe that's what I need. Some peyote."

He looked down at the bowl of conch in front of him and gathered some with the fork. "I'd be willing to bet that peyote burns all the way down, like this conch. Cleans your spirit, inside and out." He shoved the forkful into his mouth, savoring the experience. Then he nodded toward my bowl. "Go ahead."

I stared down at the rubbery meat, all slathered in sauce.

The back of my throat seized and my stomach started to churn acid, round and round, like an angry vortex. My whole career flashed before my eyes, ruined because I blew my cover over a bite of food. I looked up at Jesse. "It, ah, looks really hot, that's for sure." I summoned some courage and poked around with my fork.

He watched me with steady eyes.

I stabbed a tiny piece with the plastic tines and raised it to my mouth. *It's not going to kill you. Once down the hatch, it'll be okay.* "Bottoms up," I said and shoved it in before I could change my mind. The sauce was divine, I'd give him that, but when I felt the conch on my tongue, my lips pursed involuntarily. I couldn't chew. I held it on my tongue, trying not to shake. *Omigod.* If I didn't like conch, why else would I be at a conch shack?

I'm such an idiot. I should've sent Tom. That man was like Mikey, he'd eat anything.

Okay, man up, McVie. You're a federal agent, for godsake.

With my hand wrapped around the bottle of Kalik, I forced myself to swallow, then gulped down half the bottle.

"Yep, that's—" I rubbed my lips together "—that's a little hot," I lied.

He shook his head and grinned.

"I'm glad you're amused," I managed.

With three more bites, he'd emptied his bowl. "Well, it was nice talking to you, Poppy. Maybe I'll see you around," he said and rose from the table.

Dammit! Had I blown it? *Crap!* "Yes, thanks for lunch," I said to his backside.

He tossed his trash in the nearby can and crossed the street.

I picked up my bowl, still full of conch, tossed it in the trash with a silent apology to the snail who'd given his life for the cause, and followed him.

He went around the building that housed an outfitter offering fishing tours. I waited for another ten minutes, but if I didn't get back to the dock to head out with Dalton and Tom, we'd miss our window.

I called Mike and explained what I'd found. He agreed to take over the surveillance. In minutes, he arrived and I jogged back to the marina.

CHAPTER 9

Dalton had managed to borrow the Zodiac. We rigged it to a tow line to the fishing vessel and set out toward Florida, Tom at the helm.

After I'd helped stow the lines, I sat on a bench at the stern, watching the Zodiac surf on our wake. If the line broke, I wanted to know right away. Without the Zodiac, this mission would be done.

The hum of the engines and the constant motion of the boat cutting through the waves lulled me into a state of melancholy. What was I doing with this thing with Dalton? He was right. I didn't know what I wanted. And this operation felt the same way. What the hell were we doing here? Chasing the wind.

These guys probably were running drugs. But with dolphins? It seemed too improbable. And that Jesse. He didn't seem like the type. Or maybe he was. What did I know anymore? I'd lost my mojo. Usually I was pretty good at judging these things, but my own radar was on the fritz.

One night with Dalton and I can't think straight. What's happened to me?

I stared at the frothy sea, finding no answers.

Dalton sat down next to me. He took a hold of my hand and leaned in to whisper in my ear. "So, you were disappointed, that it?"

"What?" I spun to face him. "What are you talking about?"

"You know," he said, his tone serious.

"No, no," I said, shaking my head. "That's not…no!" *Are you kidding? I'm still on fire.*

He leaned back to my ear. "So, you liked it then?"

"Well, I—well, yeah." *Liked isn't the right word. More like delighted, relished, luxuriated in.*

He leaned back. "Then what's the problem?"

Good question? "There is no problem. That's what I've been trying to say."

"I don't know what you want from me, Poppy."

"Nothing. I don't want anything."

He stared at me for so long I had to look away.

The Zodiac bounced and surfed, bounced and surfed, until Tom hollered from the helm. Dalton got up and went to talk to him. I breathed again.

The boat slowed. "We're up," Dalton said, heading for the lines.

I donned my life vest and climbed into the Zodiac to start the engine before Dalton let the lines loose. Then he climbed aboard and took over at the helm.

My phone read, "no service."

"Just keep an eye on us," Dalton told Tom.

With a handheld GPS unit, Dalton found the coordinates which we'd decided would put us at the most likely crossroads and slowed. Lucky for us, I had three bars on my phone. At least we could connect with Mike back on the island.

"Now we wait," he said, killing the engine.

The sudden silence felt comforting. The sea was surprisingly calm. The sun hovered on the horizon, casting a warm glow across miles of ocean. The air was the perfect temperature. Not hot. Not cool.

I said, "Seems like the perfect evening to go skinny-dipping."

Why had I said that? I turned to see him grinning at me.

"I'm sure we have plenty of time," he said, his voice husky. "If you're in the mood."

"It was merely an observation." Now, why'd I say that?

"Right," he said, giving me no hint of his thoughts. "There might be sharks."

While I was trying to think of some clever retort, he closed the distance between us and had me in his arms. His lips on mine felt like the most natural thing in the world.

"I can't keep my hands off of you," he said between kisses.

"I can't stop thinking about having your hands on me."

The sky spun around. I gripped his shoulders and held on, giving in to the seductive power of his kiss. I should have resisted. Taken control. But it felt so damn good to be in his arms again, to let go, to be free.

When his phone rang, we startled apart, panting for air. The moon had risen—a gigantic glowing orb—its reflection sparkling across the water.

Dalton answered and put the phone on speaker mode. It was Mike. "Our guys took a skiff loaded with a pile of backpacks out to their boat."

"You see what was in them?" Dalton asked.

"No, but they pulled anchor right after dark and headed out. As soon as they left the harbor, they killed their running lights. I tracked them on the radar as far as I could and have a trajectory." He gave us the land coordinates. "Assuming he stays the course."

"Roger that," Dalton said.

"One more thing," Mike added. "Be on the ready. I did some quick math, which was never my strong point, but it seems his boat speed is higher than spec for that model, just like you suspected. He's really cruising."

Dalton disconnected and looked at me. "When you walked down the beach earlier, did you see anything?"

"I talked with a man I believe swam to shore from the boat.

Briefly. He bought me lunch at a conch shack. And a beer."

His eyebrows shot up. "You ate conch?"

"I managed to skirt that one."

"Why didn't you mention this before?"

"Why didn't you mention being married before?"

Damn. Why'd I say that?

He stared at me for a long time. Too long.

Finally, he said, "So, in this meeting, what information did you get?"

"He was nice. Too nice."

"You probably scrambled his brains with your smile."

A smile spontaneously spread across my face. "I can't picture him as a drug smuggler. But, then again, I don't know. One thing, though, he had an interesting tattoo." I described it the best I could remember.

Dalton nodded. He knew the tattoo. "Marine Force Recon."

"What's that mean?"

"It means he's a badass." But his expression made him seem more concerned than fearful.

"What are you thinking?"

"I'm not sure yet," was all he'd say.

Dalton fired up the engine and put the throttle down, heading to the coordinates Mike had given us.

My hair whipped in my face as I scanned the horizon through binoculars. After about twenty minutes passed, I finally saw something. "I can see a white line of froth." The wake left by a boat. I held up my hand and pointed in that direction.

Dalton acknowledged with a nod. He'd set a course where we'd intersect within territorial waters.

Soon, I could make out the shape of a white boat without the binoculars. "I thought we weren't going to get too close."

"I doubt they'd be suspicious. They can't expect we followed all the way from Bimini in this vessel."

"Makes sense," I said.

At that moment, the boat we were following turned to starboard, made a full one-eighty, and headed right for us.

"What are they doing?"

Dalton shook his head.

They bore down on us.

"Coming to see who's following them?"

Dalton looked concerned.

The boat came closer and closer, straight for us.

"He's coming to us," I said. "What should we say?"

Dalton never took his attention from the boat.

Within one hundred feet, the boat showed no sign of slowing. It came closer. Coming fast. He wasn't stopping. Dalton turned the wheel, but it was too late. The boat came so close, its wave lifted the Zodiac, and I was airborne. The engine whirred in my ears as I plunged underwater. My coastal life vest inflated with a pop when it hit the water, squeezing me tight, and I bobbed up like a cork.

Dalton must have been behind me. In the water with me, somewhere.

The boat spun around and came back at us again. Were they trying to kill us? They'd already disabled us. The Zodiac was upside down. I was a sitting duck. There was no way to get out of their way now.

The engine on our vessel sputtered and shut off.

The boat slowed and came alongside the Zodiac. A man standing on the flybridge shouted at me. "Who are you? What do you want?"

"What the hell, man," I shouted back. "I was just trying to get to shore." I needed a good story, and fast. Once Jesse recognized me, I'd need my story to make sense. Why didn't I think of this before?

"Right." This guy was a confident smart ass. "You feds? DEA?"

"What? No." Where was Dalton? "Didn't you see me? You've flipped my boat. I'm going to need your help getting it flipped back upright."

"Where's your partner?"

"I don't know what you mean. Please. Throw me a line. You can't leave me out here like this."

If I could get him to toss a line, or even reach out to me, I could pull him into the water, get a jump on him.

Where was Dalton? Under the Zodiac? Waiting for his moment?

The man climbed down the ladder as the boat came around. "Why were you following us?"

"I told you. I wasn't."

"Let me make some things clear, little lady. I have the high ground and you're in the water. Know how to tell if there's sharks in the water? Taste it. If it tastes salty, there's sharks in the water. So, you really need to start being a bit more forthright."

"Okay. Whatever you say. Just help me out of the water," I said.

The man leaned over the side to have a look. It was Jesse.

"What the hell?" he said, recognizing me. "What are you doing way out here?"

He stepped onto the swim platform at the stern. "It's all right, Deuce, I know her."

Something wasn't right. A glance between them. The tone of voice. Something.

Jesse reached down to haul me out. When he took my hand, I latched onto his wrist, braced both feet on the edge of the platform, shoved with my legs, and yanked him off his feet, into the water with me.

With a quick kick, I was up on the platform and rushing the other guy.

A yellow lab came at me, teeth bared.

A roar of laughter rumbled behind me. "Poppy! Stop! Stand down!"

It was Dalton.

I spun around.

He was in the water next to the Zodiac, grinning. "Deuce! What the hell, man? What are you doing in the middle of the Atlantic?"

"Dalton?" The other man said. "You gotta be kidding me." He stood with fists on his hips, an amused grin on his face.

Jesse hauled out of the water onto the swim platform with Dalton right behind him. Dalton and Deuce performed some kind of man hug, water dripping everywhere.

"What's going on?" I said.

The dog had a better clue than I did. He yipped and wagged his tail.

"Poppy," Dalton said. "This is Deuce. Formerly Lieutenant Commander Russel Livingston, Junior. He was the outgoing Team Leader when I first reported to Dam Neck."

"Commander," Deuce corrected him. "I was promoted after I left DEVGRU." He slapped Dalton on the back and gestured toward Jesse. "You might have heard of my partner Jesse McDermitt, former Marine Recon sniper. This is his boat."

"I've heard of you," Dalton said, extending his hand. "You're the Jarhead who took down a warlord in the Mog with a thousand meter shot. An honor to meet you, sir."

"Just Jesse," he said, shaking his hand. "And who is this little spark plug?" His eyes were on me. "Poppy your real name?"

"My partner, Special Agent Poppy McVie."

"Special Agent, indeed," Jesse said, one corner of his mouth turned up.

"She's the brains of the operation. I'm the brawn."

Jesse smirked. "What operation would that be that you're following us?"

"Well,"—Dalton tried to hide a sheepish grin—"we thought you might be running drugs."

Jesse smirked again. His dog came to stand beside him. "This is Finn."

I knelt and scratched the loose fur around his neck and ears. "Hiya, Finn."

Dalton turned back to Deuce. "Hey, if you've got a beer, we'll fill you in."

"That we can do," Deuce said, opening a small refrigerator. "We might feel up to flipping your boat back over for you, too."

"That'd be much appreciated," Dalton said as he accepted a stubby brown Red Stripe bottle.

I took a cold one as well and we sat down on the gunwale and told them what we were investigating.

After letting his dog inside the boat and closing the hatch, Jesse leaned on the back of a chair and said, "So, you're flying blind."

"Yep, that pretty much sums it up." Dalton drained the beer and handed him the empty bottle.

These men might have been old buddies of Dalton's, but they still had acted with suspicious behavior. "Where were you headed, anyway?" I asked. "In the middle of the night, without your running lights on?"

Jesse turned to Dalton. "You were right. The brains." He turned back to me. "Picking up a friend."

"And the lights?" I pressed.

"We were watching for dinoflagellates stirred up in this area. They're bioluminescent. It's really quite something to see."

"Right, I've heard of that," I said. *But not here. And running lights wouldn't ruin your night vision or ability to see bioluminescence in the water.*

"Hey, let's get that boat flipped back over and get you on your way," he said, moving up to the helm, his dog on his heels. The Zodiac had drifted a good fifty feet away.

"You might want to hold up a minute," Dalton said. "I, ah, I wrapped a line around your prop."

Jesse grinned with respect.

In a few minutes, Dalton had the line safely removed from the prop and our new friends had the Zodiac upright and running again.

Dalton and I boarded the vessel and waved farewell.

Jesse waved back. "We'll be back in Bimini for a few days. If we see anything, we'll let you know."

"Appreciate it," Dalton said as he pushed the throttle into gear.

CHAPTER 10

My elbow was the color of an eggplant—from what, I had no idea. Probably whacked it on the windshield when I ejected from the Zodiac. My dad always seemed to have weird bruises. He'd laugh and say they were clues about what his body was doing while he was in the trance of shooting. His pictures were magnificent. Seeing animals through his lens was an experience. *What were you shooting, Dad, in your last moments in Africa?*

As I held a bag of ice on my own battle scar, I stared out over the marina to the mangroves beyond. It was my day off. From my intern duties, that is. A good thing because I didn't get to bed until four a.m.

I didn't envy Dalton having to explain the damage to the Zodiac. Of course, his boss knew from the beginning that he was here undercover. And the government would cover the damage. But still.

And this morning, we knew nothing more than we did before.

We were back to square one.

The more I thought about it, the more I didn't buy the drug running theory anyway. There had to be some other connection, some other reason to train a dolphin to carry a backpack. But filled with what, pirate treasure? Follow the money. That's what they say. Bimini had a long history of pirates and shipwrecks, not to mention looting. Had someone trained dolphins to retrieve valuables from deep-water shipwrecks? Maybe, but the dolphins couldn't load the backpacks themselves, but they could transport the goods. Maybe. Seemed far-fetched still.

Follow the money...

Skylar planned to study the impact of the building of the pier—the pier where the express ferry docked, bringing hordes of spenders to the casino at the Hilton. Was there some tie there? Possibly. But the casino was open for business. Nothing was hindering it, as far as I could tell. Maybe something was in the works that would hinder it.

"There you are," Chris said, approaching me. "What are you doing?"

"I'm sitting in a bright pink Adirondack chair on a tropical island, enjoying the ocean breeze. I just ordered a drink with an umbrella in it."

"Oh-kay. What's happened?"

I told him about the midnight run that went nowhere.

"Wow, that sucks."

"Yeah."

My drink arrived. Chris grabbed it before I had a chance and slurped a mouthful through the straw. "Maybe you're going about this all the wrong way."

I sat up in the chair and took the drink from him. "Do you know how many plastic straws are used every day?"

"No. Did you hear me?"

"Yes. I'm sure I am." I yanked the drink from his hand and took a sip. "What would you do? I mean, if you could train a dolphin to do anything, anything in the world, specifically carry something, what would it be?"

He thought about it for a moment. "I'd train one to knit."

"I'm serious."

"I am too. Maybe attach the knitting needles to their flippers somehow, and then—"

"All right, you're right. I'm going to order another drink. Without a straw."

"My point is, you don't seem to be thinking outside of the box here."

"I know. I told you. My brain's been fried."

His eyebrows wiggled up and down. "Hot, steamy sex will do that."

I sighed. "Yeah, so does meeting his ex-wife the very next day."

"What! Are you serious? Did you even know he—"

"No." I glanced around, making sure no else could hear us.

"And what, she just showed up? Here?"

"On her honeymoon. And she's pregnant. Married to an old friend of Dalton's, a SEAL." I frowned. "They were on the dolphin swim."

"No way. What an odd coincidence."

I stared at Chris. It was an odd coincidence. "Well, she told me she's always loved dolphins. This is one of the best places in the world to swim with them in the wild."

"So what'd he say about it? Why has he never told you?"

"You know Dalton."

"I can't believe you didn't tell me this before."

I shrugged. "I've had a lot on my mind. Do you think my dad would have liked Dalton?"

"Whoa, okay, switching gears. What brought that up?"

"I don't know, rum?" I took another sip. "I was just thinking about Dalton being married before and what that would be like and my dad will never walk me down the aisle, which is fine because all of that is really not my style anyway."

"Okay, Poppy-girl, you really need a break."

"Not until I figure out why we're here on this island. The dolphins need us but I can't figure out what we're supposed to be doing. It's so frustrating!"

Chris stared at me, worried, then patted my leg. "I'm here to help. Let's focus on the job right now. I'll help you brainstorm. What are you thinking?"

I took another sip of my drink. "Well, the idea of pirates crossed my mind."

"Ooooh. Pirates." His gaze turned inward. "I saw this pirate calendar once." He pursed his lips and an eyelash fluttered.

"Are we talking about gay pirate porn?"

"No." He shook his head. "Dolphins finding treasure. I could see that."

"Yeah, but they don't have the opposable thumb needed to pick it up."

"Right."

"It could be some rich guy wanting exotic pets. There's a Saudi sheik with a fleet of gold-plated cars, I'm not kidding, who drives around London with his pet cheetah riding shotgun."

Chris groaned.

"Well, you said to think out of the box. Maybe there is some yahoo here who wants some pet dancing dolphins and the marks are from the elastic tugging too tight on their pink tutus. Who knows?"

"Not that far out of the box."

"You never know what we might stumble on to."

"Why do you have to stumble? Someone on this tiny island knows something. Who else have you talked to? About the dolphins?"

I thought about it. "No one, really."

"Exactly."

"Okay, Sherlock, what do you suggest?"

He cocked his head, eyed me.

"Yeah, sorry. I don't know why I'm being snarky. I'm just…"

"Maybe you do need the day off."

"No. Tell me your idea. Please."

"Well, there's this place called the Dolphin House. Maybe the owner has some insight."

I got up from the chair. "Sure. Why not?"

Chris helped me drain the glass, then we walked the few blocks to the most well-known tourist stop on the island.

Since 1993, Ashley Saunders, a Bahamian writer and historian, has been at work building the Dolphin House—a kind of museum-tribute—by hand, with only recycled materials he's found on the island and in the sea.

The exterior facade is a sandy stucco embedded with rows of conch shells, mosaics made of broken tiles of all colors, fossilized coral, and any other one-of-a-kind item he felt added to the charm, like a plastic seahorse or broken wine bottle.

Inside, the decor is just as eclectic. Every color of the rainbow shines from the multiple mosaics on each wall, representations of all kinds of scenes from the sea. License plates from all over the world are embedded along the ceiling like a wallpaper border. Fishing net and floats hang from the rafters.

One wall sports a whiskey bottle embedded in the concrete that still has one shot left in the bottom. Ashley had a story for that and every other embellishment, including a solid bronze mermaid he'd found while swimming as a child.

On the first floor, one room is stuffed to the gills with memorabilia. Photos of famous people who've visited the island—most notably, Ernest Hemingway—as well as other historic items such as old cannon balls from the pirate era.

While he most definitely was a man obsessed with dolphins, he didn't seem particularly knowledgeable about the current state of affairs with the nearby pod. His passion was of more of a spiritual nature.

We thanked him for the tour and gave a donation.

As we left the building, I noticed a man sitting on the side of the road at the corner of the property of the Dolphin House.

His hair hadn't been combed in some time. He wore a green army jacket decorated in patches and threadbare shorts.

I approached, said hello.

"They'll take ya ta mars," he muttered.

"What? Who will?" I asked.

"Dolphins. They kin teleport ya. It's all interstellar, man."

I gave Chris a subtle nod to keep walking, not to crowd us, and sat down in the shade next to the man. "The dolphins? They travel to Mars?" I asked. He clearly did not have full, neurotypical brain function, but you never know where you might get a bit of information. "How do they do that?"

He shrugged. "Dunno. Gov'ment secret. But they kin, just the same. Beam ya up, Scotty. In a hollow-gram."

"That's fascinating," I said. "I didn't realize they could form holograms."

"Everybody knows that." He picked at the hem on his shorts.

"Have you ever done it?" I asked him, trying not to make him feel like I was interrogating him. He seemed like he'd clam up.

"What'sat?"

"Teleported to Mars?"

He shook his head. "Ya gots to be careful. It's dangerous."

"What's dangerous?"

His eyes locked on mine, crazy eyes. "Messing wit what the gov'ment don't want ya to know no how."

He had a thing about the government. My bet was he was a troubled veteran. "Do *you* know the secret the government doesn't want us to know?"

"Tis them Ruskies. They invading."

"I see," I said. "And the dolphins? Are they—?"

My phone rang in my pocket.

The man's eyes narrowed. He pursed his lips. "I don't know nothin'."

"Okay, I understand," I said, getting to my feet. "It was nice to talk to you."

He didn't acknowledge my goodbye.

It was Greg calling. I put the phone to my ear as I walked away. "Yo. Can't you tell, with your fancy computer skills, when it's a bad time to call?"

"Nope. You ever heard of muting your phone?"

"Touché."

"Yeah, so I came across an anomaly. Missing file numbers."

"You lost me."

"The homework you ditched. The photo filing of the dorsal fins. There's a segment of files missing."

"How do you know they're missing? I mean, if they're missing, how can you know, you know?"

"Because I'm a genius."

"Well, that's a given. But, uh, I need the layman's explanation."

"The numbers are missing from the sequence. Even photos that are out of focus or of someone's feet get filed. They go in a dump folder. It's a science thing. You don't delete. Just label unusable, or whatever."

"Okay, I remember her telling me that."

"But there's a whole section of deleted photos. Gone. Disappeared."

"Let me guess, the dates start about eight weeks ago." The timeframe in which Skylar said the dolphins had first arrived.

"Yep."

It was time to have a talk with Kerrie.

"You're welcome," he said and hung up.

CHAPTER 11

Kerrie's home was a one-story bungalow on the south end of the island, facing the sea. We found her on a plastic lawn chair in the shade, watching her kids play in the sand.

She rose from the chair to greet us. "You're back? So sorry for your loss."

I'd forgotten to fill Chris in on my cover story, how I'd explained my trip to Mississippi with a dead grandfather. He was quick enough to follow along.

"Thank you," I said. "This is my friend, Chris. He's just visiting for a couple days."

"As long as you get the work done," she said with a not-so-friendly tone. Maybe she wanted me to be a little distracted, not dig too deep. No such luck, lady.

"Not a problem." *Some intern at headquarters is plugging away at it right now.* "That's what I came to talk to you about."

She crossed her arms, holding herself still, but her eyes flitted from me to Chris and back.

"Something's been bugging me. I was logging the photos, like you asked, and there are some files missing."

She blinked, trying to hide her reaction. "What do you mean, missing? If they're missing, how would you know they're missing?"

Exactly what I said. "Digital photos are given a file name in numerical sequence as they're taken. There's a whole bunch missing."

She shrugged, looking away. "They were probably bad photos. Got deleted. Forget about it. Just focus on the ones that are there."

"Well, see, I thought of that. But then I remembered that you told me to file every image, even those out of focus or whatever. You told me specifically not to delete them."

She glared at me. "Even scientists make mistakes. Don't worry about it."

"Are you sure, because—"

"Yes, I'm sure," she snapped and moved toward her kids. Over her shoulder, she said, "Go on now."

Chris and I followed.

"I noticed another thing," I said, acting as if her behavior was perfectly normal.

She drew in a breath and exhaled with annoyance. "Yes?"

"There aren't any photos of the dolphin that got stranded. Or the one that came up to the boat the other day."

Her muscles tensed.

I continued. "The ones with the satellite trackers on their dorsal fins."

She spun on me. "Listen. I've given you a really simple task. Catalog the photos that are there, not waste time wondering this and that. Now, can you do that or not?"

Her eyes flashed. She was scared. As sure as the sky was blue, there was fear in her eyes. She definitely knew something. Something big. And there was no way she was going to tell me, an intern.

Had she been threatened? I glanced down at her kids. She had a lot to lose.

A thought bubbled up in my brain. The man who'd been following me. He *had* been following me. Had he threatened Kerrie? He wasn't Bahamian. Or an American. His facial features were European. Definitely Eastern bloc. Belarusian came to mind.

Then I remembered something the homeless veteran had said. *Could it be?*

"I can do the job," I said. "It's not a problem."

Relief showed in her eyes.

"But I do have one more question."

She tensed again.

"I met this man over by the Dolphin House. He told me dolphins can teleport to Mars."

She snorted and seemed to relax slightly. "You can't be serious."

"Yeah, no." I smiled. "But he also said something not so crazy. He said the Russians were invading."

Her face paled. Barely, but enough that I noticed. She gathered her son close to her and her eyes locked onto her daughter. "That's a troubled old man," she said, keeping her voice steady. "I don't know why you're wasting your time. Please just do your job."

Chris and I nodded and headed back toward the office. Once we were far enough away, I asked Chris, "What do you think?"

"As sure as I know you're head-over-heels in love with Dalton, I'm sure that woman has been threatened by a Russian."

I clamped my jaw tight.

I called another meeting of the team.

This time, we met right away. I filled them in.

"Why didn't you mention this Russian guy before?" Mike said, a hint of accusation in his voice.

"Hey," Dalton said. "We already chased one red herring."

Mike clammed up.

"Wait, we saw a guy, looked Russian," Tom said. He turned to Mike. "Remember? On that boat, kinda looked like a live-aboard research vessel." He gave the description. "We haven't seen him in the marina at all though."

"We could take some jet skis, zoom around like tourists, get a look at it," I suggested.

Dalton shook his head. "You're too recognizable with that red hair."

I frowned. It was true. If I was right, and he'd been following me, he knew who I was.

Mike said, "We could take *Droppin' Skirts* out near him, do some fishing, maybe barbecue, check it out. I've got a sauce recipe I've been wanting to try that's—"

"You're enjoying this op a little too much," I said. "Especially the whole *dropping skirts* thing."

Tom held back a smirk.

"Hey, did I mention the two blondes in bikinis we met? We could get them to come along, too, maybe ride on the bow. Perfect distraction. They'll never notice there are two dudes on board."

Eye roll.

"I'll take care of it," Dalton said and got up to leave.

"Wait." I got up to follow him. "How? What do you mean?"

"I'll take care of it."

I waved a quick goodbye to the guys and followed him down the dock.

"Hey, wait."

He didn't slow or look back.

"Dalton!"

He stopped but didn't turn.

I came up beside him. "What the hell?"

A flock of gulls launched from the dock in a flutter of wings, yack, yack, yacking.

"What's going on? Since when do you go off and do something without informing your team?"

"This one—" He sighed. "I can get what we need. It'll just have to be off book."

"Off book? What are you talking about? You don't do things off book."

"I'm a SEAL, remember? I know how to board his vessel without him knowing I was there."

"Right. So, why couldn't you tell me and the guys?"

"It's a two man job."

"Okay, fine. Tell me what I need to do."

He stared at me for a long moment. "Two SEALs."

"Do you think I'm not—" *Oh.* I drew back. "You're going to ask Rod?"

"He'll do it."

"I don't doubt it. But isn't that rather awkward? He's on his honeymoon for heaven's sake."

"Yeah."

"With your ex-wife."

He didn't hide his annoyance.

"Dalton. I don't understand. Why would you even—"

"Hey, there's the guys." He gestured at a boat. It was *Gaspar's Revenge*, idling toward the gas dock.

We hurried over to catch the dock lines.

"You made it back in one piece, I see," Deuce said with a grin.

The dog jumped up and braced his front legs on the gunwale and greeted me with his tail wagging side to side. I scratched his ears.

Jesse killed the engines and directed the dockhand where to fill his tanks, then joined us on the dock. "How's the investigation going?"

"We've got another lead," Dalton said. "I was just heading over to recruit Whit. He's here on the island."

"Rod Whitaker?" Deuce asked. "He's here?"

"Yeah," Dalton said. "On his honeymoon."

Deuce glanced at Jesse and some shared bit of knowledge passed between them.

"Whatcha need?" Jesse asked.

"Need to board a vessel. No footprint."

Jesse gazed out over the boats anchored in the bay. "We're just killing time for a day or two. Need any help?"

"Could be like the old days," Deuce added.

Dalton nodded. "Yeah. That'd be great. But I still need Whit."

"Didn't you say he's on his honeymoon?"

"Yeah, but the boat, we think they're Russian."

Deuce nodded in understanding. "Roger that. C'mon aboard. Let me show you some gear we've got that might be what we need."

We followed him aboard and stepped up into a salon that belied the boat's charter fishing exterior. It was done in a subdued white, with light colored wood accents and tan leather. Very luxurious.

"Have a seat," Jesse offered, sweeping a hand toward an L-shaped couch on the port side. "Care for a beer?"

He and Deuce shared another glance, and again, there seemed to be an exchange of ideas, with only the slightest of a raised eyebrow or head nod.

Dalton trusted these men, without question. But something was going on that they weren't sharing.

To Jesse, I said, "Hey, uh, Dalton said you were in the Mog. That's Mogadishu, right? Africa."

He nodded. "Yeah."

"How long were you there?"

"Too long," he replied. "As soon as the wheels of the plane touch down, you've been in that hell-hole too long."

"You ever spend any time around South Sudan?" That's

where my dad died. Killed by poachers. Maybe he would have some insight.

He looked to Dalton, then back to me. "Not officially."

Dalton cleared his throat. "Not now, Poppy."

What? Had I stumbled on some code among brothers? Don't ask kinda thing?

Jesse leaned against the Corian countertop that separated the lounge from the galley. He fixed Dalton with his piercing blue eyes. "Deuce says you're good-to-go, Dalton. That's good enough for me. Under the bench Poppy's sitting on, I have three Draeger PSS 7000s, all charged, inspected, and ready to go."

Dalton let out a slow whistle. "Wish we had your funding."

"Personal gear," he said, one corner of his mouth coming up in a half grin. "I can also add noise-makers, if you're not carrying."

"We're good there," Dalton said. "And I have access to some gear at the dive shop, too. But, um, just out of curiosity, what kind of noise-makers."

Jesse gave Dalton another half grin. "Ma Deuce is below your seat."

"No way! How?"

"Custom built titanium tripod that fits into the fighting chair's deck receiver. Got some full auto long guns, and plenty of pistols and ammo. In case of an apocalypse, there's an electric mini-gun, as well."

Dalton didn't show much reaction, but I could tell he was impressed with the hardware. He spread a paper chart out on the settee. The Russian boat was anchored half a mile northeast of the northern tip of the island. They discussed an entry point four miles up the coast from where we were. It was a desolate beach way past Bailey Town, just before the islands' northern point.

Carrying tactical type dive gear, on foot, after midnight, was out of the question. Dalton said he could get a golf cart and a couple of seabags to carry the gear.

"I appreciate the equipment and backup," Dalton said. "But this—"

"Your op," Deuce said. "You call the shots. Jesse and I can provide the equipment and help you get there. But we're just backup. We'll stay in the water."

Dalton grinned. "Thanks, Deuce."

In minutes, the three men had put together a plan—one that obviously didn't include me.

"Hey, what about me?" I said.

Deuce shook his head.

Jesse crossed his arms. "Nope," was all he said.

"What do you mean, nope? This is my op. Dalton and I are partners."

"Yeah, no," Jesse said, looking to Dalton.

The heat rose up my neck. I could feel it setting my skin on fire.

Dalton held up his hand. "Poppy, listen. It's nothing personal."

"Right. It's just a *guy* thing?" My eyeballs were starting to bulge.

"No, no." He shook his head. "No. It's a military thing. They're not comfortable with you because they don't know you like I do, that's all. These men have trained together, fought together."

I held my ground. "We've fought together."

Dalton took me by the arm and whispered in my ear, "I'll ditch them and take you if you can tell me what 'Ma Deuce' is."

I stared back at him. He knew I had no idea.

He said aloud, "Ma Deuce is an affectionate term for the M-2 fifty-caliber machine gun, developed by Browning in the 1930s to destroy tanks. It's still employed today."

"Men and their gadgets," I said, trying to sound

unimpressed.

Jesse and Deuce stared at me, smug.

"Yeah, well, what am I supposed to do? Hang out here and babysit Finn?"

"Finn can take care of himself," Jesse said. Then he winked at me. "You're welcome to hang out on the boat, looking pretty. That's something you seem to excel at."

The needle shot off the scale. "Would you like to spend the rest of your life speaking in a falsetto voice?"

He turned to Dalton. "Wow, she is quite the little spark plug. You got your hands full, don't you buddy?"

"You don't know the half of it," Dalton muttered.

"What? You don't like your normal speaking voice either?"

He clamped his mouth shut.

CHAPTER 12

"I was hoping we'd be able to see from here," I said to Alison, pulling behind some tropical foliage near the beach. To our left a topless golf cart was parked on the dune, a hundred yards from where the beach turned around the northern tip of the island. I assumed it was the one Dalton had borrowed.

He wouldn't like it very much if he knew I was here. Well, too bad. Sitting on the sidelines wasn't exactly my style. Turns out, it wasn't Alison's either. She'd demanded that I bring her along.

We sat in our hidden golf cart, facing the ocean. The sun had set hours ago, but I had night vision binoculars trained on the boat anchored offshore. There were no stars. No moon. Clouds had been moving in all day.

"You won't see them. They're SEALs," she said, clasping her handbag tightly to her belly. "That's the point."

"Yeah, but *we* know they're there."

She shrugged, as if that didn't matter.

"I should be out there with him." *Not here. Watching. Waiting. Worthless.*

Where were they now? They're plan was to swim from shore, board the vessel in the dark, get whatever intel they could, and head back. All without being detected. Child's play for a team of Navy SEALs.

"I have to be honest," Alison said. "This wasn't exactly how

I thought I was going to be spending the evening."

"I'm sorry. I told Dalton not to—"

"Don't be. I know who I married." She let out a little laugh. "Both times. *Hooyah*."

"Dalton told me you didn't like being a Navy wife."

"That part's true."

There was a long awkward silence. I held up the binoculars, but saw nothing. Not a ripple on the surface.

It really wasn't my business. Whatever had happened between them, Dalton would tell me. Or he wouldn't. If I was honest, I didn't have a right to know. It wasn't like we were… whatever. Was he my boyfriend? *I don't know.*

"I'm glad we have this time together to talk," she said.

Talk?

"Because I know one thing for sure," she said with a soft voice. "Dalton's madly in love with you."

My tongue glued to the roof of my mouth. "Oh, I don't think—"

"Pah," she said, sweeping my words away with her hand. "I've known that man since first grade. Believe me. As sure as the sun sets every night, he's head-over-heels. I can feel it."

I clamped my mouth shut. I had no idea what the appropriate response was when a man's ex-wife said such a thing.

"I'm so happy for him. For you. I've been worried that maybe he wouldn't ever let himself fall in love again."

In love? "Well, I don't…"

"You're a very lucky lady. You know that, right? Very lucky indeed."

"Yeah, but…"

"He's a good man. They don't make 'em like Dalton every day, that's for sure."

A flash of light flickered across the sky. "Was that lightning?"

"I don't know."

I looked at my watch. 1:30 a.m. "They should be back by now."

"I'm sure they're fine," she said, but her voice revealed her concern.

"They didn't give us an exact time."

"Right. They never do," she said. "I'd be lying if I didn't admit it makes me sad, you know."

"What makes you sad? Worrying about them?"

"Huh? No. That Dalton's in love." She fiddled with her handbag. "I've loved him for as long as I can remember. And I know he loved me, too. But, we grew up. Grew apart. Sometimes love ain't enough, you know." She looked up, forced her hands to stop. "Dalton, he wanted to be part of something bigger than himself. Make a difference. I just wanted to go home." She paused. "I guess you could say, we just weren't in sync. I never could understand why he wanted to be a SEAL, why he'd put himself in such dangerous situations. He couldn't just be with me. His mind was always someplace else." She looked back down at her hands. "I'm sure he told you what happened."

He didn't tell me you existed.

"I hope you don't judge me too harshly. He was gone so much. And sometimes, I had no idea where, for how long. Whether he'd even make it back. It was hard. Then trying to get him to talk to me, to share anything he was feeling…"

"I understand," I said. Was she saying—?

"It's not me. It's not who I am. It just happened. I don't know what I was thinking. I just…" She shook her head. "I was so lonely."

I sat still, not wanting any more words to spill out of her. I had wanted to learn what I could about Dalton, about their relationship, this marriage I didn't know existed. Now, I felt like I'd invaded his privacy. Her privacy.

I picked up the binoculars again, looked out at the dark

ocean. Away from her. "They'll be back any minute."

"I'm sure he still hates me."

The way she said it made it sound like a question. "I don't know anything about that," I said. This woman had broken my Dalton's heart. Did he hate her? He didn't seem to.

Light flashed across the sky again. Where were they?

"We agreed, things happen for a reason. We wanted different things but neither one of us wanted to admit it. It's not like we fought all the time or anything like that. We just, well, once we were adults, we weren't compatible." She heaved a sigh and sat back. "Now, I've found Rod. And Dalton's found you. I'm so happy. I really am." She tugged my arm. "Poppy, promise me you won't break his heart."

I turned to face her. "What?"

"Promise me. He deserves someone who loves him, truly loves him, for who he is. With all your heart, promise me."

"Well, I—we aren't even—I mean—"

She looked forlorn. "He loves you. Don't tell me you aren't in love with him, too?"

"It's not that, I—"

"Well, what?" Her voice cracked. "Either you love him or you don't."

"I do." *Omigod, what is wrong with me? Did I just say that? To her?*

"I knew it," she said, as if I'd just admitted to having red hair. She grinned. "You two are so right for each other."

Like fire and gasoline.

One hour later than I expected, the men emerged from the water and came ashore carrying their fins in their hands.

We weren't supposed to be here but Allison immediately blew our cover. She raced toward Rod and if he was surprised he didn't show it, just swooped her up in his big arms.

Freaking civilians.

Dalton wasn't surprised to see me either, in fact, he looked downright amused. If he thought I was going to throw myself in his arms like a pining sea-wife he had another thing coming. I crossed my arms.

"How'd it go? What was the delay? Are you all right? Of course, you're all right, you look very pleased with yourself."

"You were worried about me?" he said with a grin. "I didn't mean to keep you waiting."

"Well, yeah. I mean, no. Of course there was no need to worry. I just—yeah, you're late."

His grin got a little wider. He wiped water from his forehead and ran his fingers through his hair, brushing it back from his face. "We got the right boat. They're definitely our guys. Buckets of fish and shrimp on board. Two men. Russians. And interestingly, military."

"Military?" That was a surprise.

I looked to the others. Jesse and Deuce walked toward the topless cart, shedding gear as they went.

Rod nodded his head, dropping his rebreather onto the back of the other golf cart. "I'm sure of it. They had military communication equipment and the documents I saw, their directive, most definitely in military format."

"What was the directive?"

"Well, they sent an update. 'Four responding to calls. Number five refusing to engage. Abort? Leave number five?' The response was to leave no evidence. They have three days to get the fifth dolphin to respond, or they are to destroy it and leave the area."

"And when was that?"

Dalton and Rod answered simultaneously. "Yesterday."

"What in the world is the Russian military doing in The Bahamas training dolphins?"

Rod and Dalton glanced at each other, then shook their heads. If they had a guess, they didn't say anything.

CHAPTER 13

I fired up the computer in the research office with Dalton looking over my shoulder.

The old monitor blinked, then slowly came to life.

"You know what this means, right?" I said.

"What?"

"I'm not paranoid. I was being followed. And the fact that the Russians can hack at that level—"

"We still don't know that that's what happened."

"Yeah, but, maybe we should call in," I said while the ancient computer made humming noises.

"And say what?"

"Tell Hyland about the Russian military."

"Yeah, but, tell her what? She'll want to know what they're doing, and why? We don't have that yet."

"Yeah, but—"

"Just see what we can find out here first." He pointed at the monitor, now blue and displaying the menu bar.

I opened the internet browser and typed in "Russian military dolphins." Right away, an article came up titled, *Crimean Military Dolphins to Serve in Russian Navy*.

The article was dated 2014. Apparently, the Russians had a military dolphin training program in Ukraine. The Ukrainian navy planned to disband it, but the facility and the dolphins themselves reverted to Russia with the reunification of Crimea.

"Reunification? That's a stretch."

He pointed at the URL. "It's Sputnik News."

"Okay, so why are they here?" I said, covering my yawn with my hand. It was 2:30 a.m.

"Keep reading."

The article said, "The dolphins were being trained to patrol open water and attack or attach buoys to items of military interest, such as mines on the seafloor or combat scuba divers trained to slip past enemy security perimeters, known as frogmen."

I turned to Dalton. "They're training dolphins to fight Navy SEALs?"

"That's what it says."

"Did you know about that?"

He shook his head. "I had no first-hand knowledge, no. But it's nothing new. During the Cold War, Russia used dolphins for military purposes. They trained them to detect submarines, flag mines, and protect ships and harbors. But so do we."

I sat back and stared at him in disbelief. "I didn't know that."

"Well, it hasn't been a secret. The U.S. Navy Marine Mammal Training Program started in the 1960s. It was in San Diego and—"

"Wait, you said *was*."

"I heard they were ending the program in 2017."

"Did they?"

"I don't know."

"What *do* you know?"

He raised an eyebrow, but continued. "That, at one point, they had something like 150 trained dolphins and around 50 sea lions. They've worked with seals, too. And other animals."

"But that's not ethical," I said. "To enlist dolphins against their will to—"

"It's the Navy," he said, as if that explained it all. "Dolphins' echolocation abilities are infinitely more sophisticated than our best sonar. They can find mines, alert us to enemy swimmers in the water. Nothing matches their abilities. At least not yet."

"Yeah, but using dolphins for war, that's—"

"I know." He pointed at the monitor. "Keep searching."

"Okay, Mr. Bossy."

His eyes met mine. "You like that?"

I flushed. "Oh, stop." I turned back toward the monitor.

Another article, posted in 2016, confirmed, "Earlier this month, the Russian government announced it was looking to buy five combat dolphins: two females and three males, physically unblemished, and in possession of 'perfect teeth.' Naturally, Russia did not reveal what it planned to do with the dolphins."

I couldn't believe it. The information was right in front of us, courtesy of Google. "These must be those same five dolphins," I said.

"Odds are, yes," Dalton replied.

The monitor flickered and went out, then came back on.

"The storm," I said. "We probably learned all we're going to from the internet anyway." I thought for a moment. "But why are they here? In The Bahamas? This country has no relationship with Russia. Does it?"

"Try one more search," he said. "Try Bahamas and Russia relations."

I did. Turns out, in 2006, the Bahamian government invested hundreds of millions in Russia, which prompted an investigation into the relationship between Bahamian officials, money laundering and the Russian mafia.

"Well, what does that have to do with training military dolphins here?"

"I don't know. But, in the morning, we need to have a real talk with your new boss. I'm betting she has some more insight for us."

"Agreed."

"Meanwhile…" He pulled my hair back from my neck and kissed me right behind my ear.

I shivered. "That's probably…we shouldn't…"

"We shouldn't what?"

His warm breath tickled my neck.

"I don't think…"

"You don't think what?" He reached across me, grabbed the armrest on the chair, and spun me around. "Don't give me that excuse about getting distracted."

He took my hand in his and pulled me to my feet, then placed his other hand at the small of my back and pulled me tight up against him. "Because we're professionals."

"We really should head to bed," I said, not really meaning it.

He grinned. "Yes, we should."

"I mean, get some sleep."

"Oh that." He leaned closer and kissed my neck. I sucked in my breath. "Sleep is overrated," he whispered.

Then he was kissing me and I knew I wasn't going to get any sleep at all.

Oh what the hell.

And I was lost in his kisses.

Dalton and I arrived at Kerrie's house, right at eight a.m. The rain battered the island in sheets. Wind whipped in off the ocean at forty miles an hour.

"You know Dalton, from the dive boat," I said as we stood in the doorway, dripping on the tile.

Kerrie invited us in. Natalie, her research assistant was there. Piles of notebooks were spread over the kitchen table. Her husband was gone, she said, working on a boat engine, and she and Natalie were catching up on some work.

"I hate to interrupt," I said, "but it's important."

She looked at Natalie. Was that an eye roll?

I reached into my pocket and presented my I.D. badge. "I'm a U.S. Federal agent. Dalton is my partner."

She jerked back from the badge in my hand as though I were holding a live snake.

"Holy crap," said Natalie. "U.S. Agents?" She looked at Kerrie with big eyes.

The blood drained from Kerrie's face and she started to wobble. Dalton was there, taking her by the arm and sitting her down in a chair.

"You're upset," I said, "but not surprised."

She shook her head, her lip quivering.

"You know about the Russian dolphins."

Her eyes moved to her children, playing in the next room. Billy pushed a fire truck around a furniture leg. Charlotte sat on the couch, her chubby legs out in front of her, brushing her doll's hair. Tears welled up in Kerrie's eyes and started streaming down her cheeks.

"It's all right," I said. "We can protect you. If you tell us everything. But you need to tell us what you know."

Natalie sat back in her chair. "Hoh-lee crap."

Dalton found a roll of paper towels and handed it to Kerrie. She thanked him with a nod, tore a sheet off the roll, and dried her eyes.

My focus on Kerrie, I went on. "You were threatened, weren't you?"

She managed a nod.

"The kids?"

She closed her eyes tight, trying to hold back the tears, then finally nodded.

My fists clenched and unclenched. How dare they? Threatening to harm her kids was viscious, the lowest of lows. I wanted to march straight out to their boat right now and slam those men against a wall.

I took a breath before saying, "Okay. Let's start at the beginning. You first saw the Russian dolphins about eight weeks ago, correct? When Skylar was the intern here?"

She nodded, then her eyes snapped up to meet mine. "Wait, how do you know about Skylar?"

"I'm an investigator. That's what I do."

"Oh." It took a moment for her to adjust to my role change before she went on. "I didn't think much about it. The dolphins, I mean. We spot transient dolphins once in awhile. Especially bottlenose that follow the coast."

"But?" I coached.

"But these had transmitters. It's customary to report sightings to the researcher. But I couldn't find any published research for these particular animals."

"Then what?"

"Then we kept seeing them, every day. They'd come up to the boat. Their behavior was odd, nothing I'd seen before."

"So, you started to suspect something?"

"It was Natalie, actually."

I turned to Natalie.

"Well, I'd done an internship at a captive facility. Their behavior reminded me of those dolphins. But still, we didn't think…"

"We hadn't heard of any errant dolphins, so I put out a notice," Kerrie said, "in the marine mammal community. It's happened before—"

"Captive dolphins getting out of their enclosures, you mean," I said. "Like over in Gulfport during Hurricane Katrina."

"Yeah," she said, surprised I knew about that, too. "I posted notice on a science forum. The next day, a man cornered me. He said to make it disappear or—" she shook, her lip trembled "—or my kids would disappear."

"And this man, he was Russian?"

She nodded, then shook her head, then nodded again. "He had a heavy accent. I think Russian, yes."

"Was he in the crowd the other day, on the beach, where the one was stranded?"

"Yes, he was there."

"Okay. Do you have any idea why they'd be here? In The Bahamas?"

Kerrie hesitated.

"Do you have a guess?" I pressed.

Natalie spoke up. "We came up with a hypothesis. We think they came from Cuba. Perhaps they were training there and the dolphins either escaped from a pen or maybe they were working with them in the open ocean. If it was illegal, whatever they were doing with the dolphins, their escape wouldn't have been made public."

"Not on the public forums?"

"Right."

"Why Cuba? Because the man who threatened you is Russian, you assumed—"

"No," Natalie said. "We came to that conclusion before he came into the picture. We looked at migratory patterns. These dolphins likely followed a wild pod of migrating dolphins from the south and Cuba is the only country where dolphins could be captive where we wouldn't have access to information about it."

"You think these dolphins escaped and made friends with some wild, migrating dolphins who—"

"More like, followed. To say they built relationships would be presumptive."

"Okay, they followed. Then once they arrived here in Bahamian waters, they decided to stay?"

She nodded. "It's prime habitat. Our dolphin population is healthy. Food supply is good. It's a dolphin paradise."

"And now their trainers are here, too. We assume they

followed them by using the satellite trackers."

They both nodded.

I thought about it all for a moment. It made perfect sense.

"Are these dolphins able to survive on their own in the wild?"

"We think so," Kerrie said. "What Natalie didn't mention, is that I did eventually find information on the internet about the Russians having purchased five dolphins a couple years ago."

"We saw that, too."

"Well, I believe they were wild-caught dolphins, not captive-born. So, yes. Though they are now in a different habitat than they were born in, we think they can survive on their own."

"And they're learning," Natalie said with excitement. "We witnessed two of them crater feeding along with a small group of our native bottlenose."

"Ah, and of all the dolphins in the world, only the Bimini dolphins have been observed crater feeding. So that's a good sign."

"A very good sign," Natalie said.

Dalton asked, "Have you seen any behavior you could identify as their trained skills?"

"I don't follow," Kerrie said.

"Is there any way to figure out what they've been trained to do?"

She shook her head. "We *briefly* witnessed them crater feeding, *once*," she said as though she felt the need to clarify Natalie's overly optimistic statement. "But that was learned behavior by watching or interacting with the wild dolphins. Other than that, they showed signs of a comfort level with humans that only comes from regular interaction. Nothing else that we've documented."

Natalie nodded her head, confirming Kerrie's statement.

"So, let me make sure I understand," I said. "It's likely

that these dolphins were being trained in Cuba, but somehow escaped, then followed some other dolphins here, wild, migrating dolphins, where they've decided to stay. The trainers have followed, using their trackers, and they don't want anyone to know about any of it, so they threatened you to keep quiet about it. That about right?"

Kerrie nodded and pushed back her bangs, glancing over to her children.

"We think so," Natalie said.

"I would think they'd want to get those dolphins out of here, back to Cuba, as soon as possible. The longer they're here, the greater the risk of being detected. I'm sure they're breaking many Bahamian laws, not to mention the international agreements on wildlife."

They nodded in agreement.

"And did you consider calling the police here? Or customs agents?"

Kerrie looked me right in the eyes. "Are you kidding? My kids…"

I nodded in understanding. The Bahamas wasn't exactly known for incorruptible police and strong federal protection. "All right. How would they do it? How would they move the dolphins back to Cuba?"

"Depends," Kerrie said, tapping her fingers on the table. "That's a long way to get them to follow staying close enough to the boat to hear the whistle calls. They'd be better to recapture them and transport them back. But they might not have the equipment for it."

"And if they can't do either?"

Dalton said, in a quiet, calm voice. "They'll cut their losses and destroy any evidence."

The room went quiet as the four of us stared at one another. We knew what that meant.

CHAPTER 14

Before we left, we assured Kerrie and Natalie that we wouldn't do anything without talking to our supervisor and to them again first.

My room was the closest. Dalton and I ran there in the pouring rain.

Once inside, I shook my raincoat in the shower. Dalton plopped down in the only chair.

"The clock is ticking for these dolphins," I said, coming out of the bathroom. Dalton's wet T-shirt clung to his chest. I bit my lip. What had I been saying? "We can't let them kill them."

"I'm not sure what we can do. We have no authority here." He combed his fingers through his hair, smoothing it back.

"Then why the hell are we here? We need to call Hyland."

"Phones are dead." He held up his hands as though he knew what I was going to say next. "But it doesn't matter. This was a seek-and-learn mission. For now, we have no other directive."

My hands squeezed into fists at my hips. "But we can't just stand by and do nothing."

He gave me that look.

"I understand, the U.S. has no authority here. That doesn't mean there's *nothing* we can do."

His eyes narrowed. "What are you thinking now?"

"I don't know." I plopped down on the edge of the bed. "We can't do anything until this storm passes." A yawn snuck up on me. "And we've been up all night."

"Yeah," he said, his eyes on me.

"But we need a plan."

"Uh-huh."

I rose and went to the window. Rain trickled down the glass in thick rivulets. A gust of wind made it vibrate. "We're stuck here. Holed up."

"Yeah, stuck. Together." He came up behind me, placed his hands on my hips. "What will we do with the time?"

My nerves buzzed. I could think of a lot of things I'd like to do. With Dalton. "You are insatiable, aren't you."

"Uh-huh."

I peeked over my shoulder.

He nuzzled my neck.

"Did you have something in mind?"

He spun me around, took hold of me by the shoulders, and said, "Yes. I think we need to talk."

Uh. What? "Fine. Let's start with why you never mentioned you had a wife."

"Ex wife."

I crossed my arms. "Either way."

"I did."

"What? You did not."

"I did. When we first met. In Costa Rica, when you barged into the bathroom—"

"I didn't *barge* in."

His eyebrows went up. "When you barged into the bathroom and demanded—"

"Oh, you mean after I asked you to fill me in on the case, you handed me that business card, told me to memorize it, and ran away into the bathroom?"

"I didn't—will you knock it off?" He waited until I

acquiesced. "In the bathroom, when you made the snarky remark about me not having a girlfriend."

I searched my memory. He'd been giving me crap about my observation skills, how the target was a rich guy, how his fat wallet was an attractive trait to women. And yes, *okay fine*, he'd said he was divorced. "I thought you were kidding."

"Why would I lie?"

"Well, you were, I mean, we had this thing, you know, our banter thing we do." I huffed. "You didn't trust me yet."

He stared at me.

"Okay, so you said it then. How was I supposed to know it was true? And that doesn't matter anyway. You've never mentioned her since. You've never told me anything about your life. Nothing. Mom, dad, brothers, sisters. Nothing. And that's fine. I know you're not a big talker, and very private, I guess. But Dalton, *a wife?*"

His shoulders slumped. He went for the edge of the bed and sat down. "It didn't come up."

"Because you didn't want to talk about what happened? Between you two?"

His eyes narrowed. "What did she tell you?"

I took the chair. "She told me she cheated on you."

He groaned, looked away. "I wish she hadn't shared that."

"I'm sorry, Dalton. That must have been—"

"Things happened the way they were supposed to."

I stared at him. "Really? That's how you feel about it? It had to have been heart-wrenching."

He shrugged. "That's how I feel about it now."

"Yeah, but—"

His eyes snapped toward mine. "What do you want me to say? Yeah, it hurt like hell. It ripped my guts out. I wanted to kill the guy." He looked away again. "He knew I was a SEAL, too, so the little prick must've had a death wish anyway."

"You knew him?"

"I don't want to talk about it."

"Okay," I said.

He stared out the window at the rain.

"She seems like she's genuinely remorseful. I think she really loved you."

"I know that," he said, his voice low.

"Well, I don't think—"

"I told you. It was a Navy marriage. I wasn't there. It is what it is. I mean, was."

"Yeah, but that doesn't—"

"But nothing." His gaze met mine. "She didn't seek it out. Yeah, I wish she would have made different decisions. But she didn't seek it out. He was my friend. A good friend. I thought. He knew I was gone, that we had some issues. He made the moves. Came on strong. End of story."

"Your *friend*?" I said, incredulous.

He looked away. "Obviously not."

"Yeah, but—"

"Poppy, really? Do we have to do this?"

"You wanted to talk."

He sighed, resigned. "It sucked. The whole situation. But it also made me see things more clearly. With her, anyway. Our relationship issues. I don't harbor any bad feelings, if that's what you're asking."

"I understand," I said.

"As for him." He winced. "Something's wrong in that man's head. A moral compass gone haywire. I don't know. I mean, who does that? I thought he was my best friend. I would have taken a bullet for him. Then, the first chance he got, he betrays me in the worst possible way. Son of a bitch kept lying to me, too. Blaming her. Saying she was all over him, like he was some kinda victim. I gave him three chances. Three times I told him, just be straight with me. But he couldn't do it. Didn't have the balls to admit what he'd done."

"I can see why you'd be angry."

"I'm not angry." He paused, thought for a moment. "I was. But not now. I pity him really. He's the one who lost. Lost my friendship, hers. Lost his integrity, if he had any to begin with. He's a pathetic creature who's probably moved on to ruin someone else's marriage."

"How'd you know the truth of what happened? I mean, they say—"

"Doesn't matter. He knows what he did. He has to live with that." He turned to look at me, finally. "Karma will take care of him."

"I'm sorry," I said. "I'm sorry all that happened to you."

He shrugged it off. "It's the risk you take when you love someone. You give that person the power to hurt you. Being in love means being vulnerable. The two go hand in hand."

He was staring at me now, with those eyes. I felt like a butterfly, pinned to the wall. Was he telling me about loving him? That I needed to let go, be vulnerable? But that's what always got me in trouble.

"That's all in the past." He rose from the bed, took my hand and pulled me to my feet. "I'm not afraid to love again. And I'm not afraid to say it. I love you, Poppy McVie."

You...what? My mouth hung open. That came right out of left field.

His eyes held mine. "I love the way your cheeks are all pink and rosy when you wake up in the morning. I love how you plunge into a mission with heart and soul, no matter the cost. Though that also drives me crazy. I love your sass. I love that you can't stand the rules." He reached up and stroked my cheek, then pushed a curl behind my ear. "You know what I love most? Your idealism. I love how you see the world with an unwavering optimism." He kissed me, ever-so-softly. My breath caught. "And if you don't want to acknowledge our relationship during an op, I'm fine with that. I can wait.

Whatever you need. All I ask is that you be honest with me, and with yourself. Tell me you love me, too."

My heart thrummed in my chest. "Well, I—I mean, it's not that—of course I—" *Love?* What was he saying? Love, as in, let's run off into the sunset? Drive away with cans tied to our bumper? Little house in the country with… little ones? With diapers and dirty faces? No. No. That's not me. I— "Aren't you worried—I mean, don't you—are you sure?"

His eyes softened with amusement. "I've never been more sure. I love you. I know you love me. Nothing else matters. If it becomes a problem with our jobs, we'll work it out."

"Yeah, but—" I slouched onto the edge of the bed. This was happening too fast. It was supposed to be just fun. Sex. Blowing off steam. That's it. Now he was throwing around the L-word. My hands started to shake. That would be, like, forever. Tied. Tethered. Like errant children.

"That's it." I shot to my feet. "The dolphins. They're tethered, by their trackers. They can never escape."

Dalton stepped back. His usual stalwart demeanor dissolved before my eyes. His eyes turned sad, and he had an expression I've never seen before. Grief? Disappointment?

"I just…"

He cocked his head to the side. "That's what comes to your mind when I tell you I love you?"

"No. Yes. I mean, I'm sorry. It's just…if we get the trackers off of them, they can truly escape."

"Right." He shoved his hands into his front jeans pockets and took another step back from me.

I stepped toward him. "It just popped into my head right then. That's all. I'm sorry. I didn't mean…it's just my brain. The way my brain works."

"Uh-huh." He stared at me for a long moment, his brow furrowed, then turned and walked out the door into the storm.

CHAPTER 15

I grabbed my raincoat from the bathroom and ran out the door after him, but he was gone.

Dammit! Why'd I say that?

Droppin' Skirts was in the marina today because of the storm. Would he go there? Or find Deuce and the guys, his old friends. He'd probably head somewhere where he could be alone. Maybe I should leave him to do that but I had to explain, make him understand.

Wind whipped my hair into my face as I ran down the street, dodging puddles, and then out onto the slippery docks. I'd check with the guys first, just in case. I had to find him. I couldn't let him think I didn't...*love him.* He'd gone and sprung it on me. That was all. How was that fair? Right out of the blue. *I love you, Poppy McVie.* What was I supposed to say? I mean, yeah, but, I don't know. It's not a word to just throw around.

Gaspar's Revenge was nowhere on the docks. I found *Droppin' Skirts* at the end of the dock. I hopped over the gunwale and pushed through the door to the salon. Dalton was aboard, sitting in the corner of the dinette with his feet up, a cup of coffee in his hand. He wouldn't look at me.

Tom eased next to me. "Coffee?"

"What?" I turned to him and suddenly realized I needed to get my head on straight. "Yeah, sure." I gestured toward

Dalton with my thumb. "Did he fill you in?"

"Not yet," he said, concern in his eyes. "He just got here." He looked from me to Dalton, then back to me. "You alright?"

"Yeah, yeah," I said. "Just…frustrated. We've only got a couple days to figure this out. And with the storm…"

A gust blew through the marina and the boat rocked in the slip. I took a seat.

"The National Weather Service is calling this the worst non-tropical storm in the Atlantic in fifty years," Mike said, pouring a cup of coffee. He handed it to me. "It doesn't have a name though." He paused. "I've never understood how that naming-thing works."

"We need to check in with Hyland," I said, then held the cup to my nose and breathed in the calming aroma of roasted Colombian beans before I took a sip.

Tom shook his head. "Phones are down. Internet. Half the island doesn't have power."

"Could be for days," Mike added.

"Well, we can't wait," I said, setting my cup down.

"Why? What's going on?"

I told them everything we knew without mentioning the SEAL team incursion. I implied Dalton went alone.

"Impressive," Tom said to Dalton.

Dalton shrugged it off.

Tom sighed. "So, what are you two thinking? What next?"

Dalton said, "This was a seek-and-learn mission. We have no other directive."

He sounded like a broken record. I swung around to face him. "But we can't just stand by and do nothing. Those dolphins are—"

"We're not going to sit on our hands and do nothing." He still wouldn't look at me. "The Navy is going to want to know exactly what the Russians have been training these dolphins to do."

"But you heard Kerrie. We have no way of knowing those things by observing the dolphins. We'd have to—"

"Capture the Russians and interrogate them." His voice was monotone.

"You're not suggesting we do that?" Tom asked, incredulous.

Dalton shook his head. "Not without an explicit directive."

"Do you think that's what we'll get?" Mike said. "When we call it in?"

"No," Dalton said, disappointment in his voice. "That would be too heavy-handed."

"What then?" Tom asked.

Dalton stared at his coffee cup, spun it side to side by the handle. "I think Hyland will want to capture the dolphins."

Mike was nodding. "Makes sense. They've already escaped. It would be believable that they slipped away. Russians might not suspect U.S. involvement at all."

Tom added, "Then Navy trainers could evaluate the dolphins, see what they can figure out."

Dalton nodded. "Shouldn't be too difficult. I'm sure we can hack the satellite transmissions to find the dolphins ourselves. We can use the acoustical equipment to listen in on their whistle calls before then."

"Wait." I couldn't believe what I was hearing. "Are you saying that you think the plan, all along, was for us to get confirmation, so the U.S. could *kidnap* the Russian dolphins, and take them to another captive facility to interrogate *them*? *The dolphins?*"

"Most likely," Dalton said, still not making eye contact.

"Well, that's not—" I shook my head. "No. These dolphins already escaped once. No way. Besides, you're making a lot of assumptions there. Kidnapping the dolphins? Without the Russians knowing? If JP and Skylar were correct, it would take a long time to train them to haul out on floating mats so they could be transported, not to mention what it would take to transport them. How could that happen with the Russians right here?"

There was an awkward silence. Then it hit me. Of course it wouldn't happen that way. The Navy handlers wouldn't bother with the training. They'd dart them, drag them aboard in nets, then hope they could resuscitate them later.

I frowned, frustrated. "Well, like I said, there's a lot of assumptions there. Maybe Hyland wants us to expose them to the Bahamians. Maybe we're supposed to put a wrench in the program, set them back, help the dolphins along in getting away. "

"And leave all that intel on the table?" Dalton shook his head. "No. This is a matter of national security. The information we get from these dolphins could save the lives of many SEALs." He finally looked me in the eye. "My brothers."

"Possibly. But it's a long shot. More likely they'll all die in transport and even if they don't, it's highly unlikely that we'd learn anything from them. Kerrie said—"

"I don't care what some civilian scientist thinks. This is way bigger than that."

My head was spinning. This couldn't be. We were an elite unit. Brought together to fight for animals. *For* animals. Not this. "It's too big of a risk for the dolphins."

"I'll take that risk," Dalton said with a fierce edge. "The lives of five dolphins over the young men and women who dedicate their lives to fight and die for this country. Hell yes."

"But we don't even know—"

"We know enough," he snapped. "That's your problem, Poppy. You can't see the big picture."

"Oh-kay," Tom said, his hands up in the air. "Let's all take a deep breath."

Dalton looked at Tom, let out his breath.

"Yeah," said Mike with a side glance at Tom. "We need to

figure out how to get a call to Hyland."

Tom leaned back on the counter. "Except we're on a remote island in the middle of the Atlantic in a tropical storm."

"We should've brought a satellite phone," Mike said.

"We can work on getting all the information compiled to report," Dalton said. "And a plan as to how we can assist. We'll need to distract the Russians somehow. We have to…"

I didn't hear any more. Dalton was making a plan to help capture the dolphins. I couldn't listen.

"Poppy, didn't you say this happened in Gulfport?" Tom asked.

"Yeah," I managed.

"We'll need any info you've got on how they recaptured those dolphins."

"Right," I said.

Dalton kept talking, planning. I couldn't believe what I was hearing.

I got up. "I need to check on something," I said and was out the door.

Three strides down the dock and Dalton was right behind me, his hand on my arm. "Hey."

I came to a halt, but didn't turn. The wind whipped at my back.

"Hey." He came around in front of me, stared into my eyes. Rain blew into his face. He didn't flinch.

I crossed my arms. "What?"

"I know it's not want you wanted to happen, but we're talking about wartime intel here."

"You're making a lot of assumptions about what Hyland would want."

"So are you. But I have more experience with—"

"Oh, you're not going to pull out that one."

His expression didn't change. "With military issues, is what I was going to say."

"We don't work for the military."

"We work for the President, Poppy. What do you think that means?"

I stared at him. Thinking. Finally I said, "I work on an elite task force, formed to investigate *animal* issues. It seems to me that maybe you're the one who's lost sight of that."

He drew in a breath to respond, but I cut him off. "We could call Hyland. With all that equipment on board *Gaspar's Revenge*, there's no doubt Jesse has a satellite phone. But you're determined to do this. You want a full plan to present to her."

He stared at me. I was right. "What if I have a different plan?"

He crossed his arms. "I guess we'll have to agree to disagree."

"I guess so. You gotta do what you gotta do. And so do I."

I pushed past him.

I leaned into the wind, holding the hood of my raincoat over my head and made for the road where I flagged down a car and asked for a ride to the Hilton.

I found Chris, sitting in the lounge, drinking a Cosmo, clicking away at his knitting.

"I've been trying to call you," he said, dropping the ball of yarn on the couch next to him as he got up. "But the phones are down."

"Power's out, too," I said. "The whole island. Except this building, of course." It was lit up like the Vegas strip.

"Sit down, sit down," he said, ushering me toward the neon green couch.

I plopped down and exhaustion came over me.

"Girl, you look like shit."

"Well, at least that's consistent with how I feel."

"What's happened? You and Dalton still doing your—"

I held up my hand. I couldn't do it. I couldn't talk about it.

"That bad, huh?" He spun around and raised his hand, waving for a server. "My friend needs a drink. Asap."

A young lady in a pressed uniform arrived, smiling. "What can I get you?"

I stared. I had no idea.

"A Bahama Mama," Chris said.

I frowned.

"Make it a double."

She nodded and retreated.

"Tell me what's happened," Chris said, sitting down next to me.

"Do I have to?"

"No. But I know you. You'll feel better."

I laid my head back, stared up at the ceiling. "I know you really want Dalton to be the one. But he's not. He's just not the one."

Chris sat back. "Okay, what's happened?"

"Nothing. He's just—he's not the guy I thought he was."

"Hogwash," Chris said. "Tell me what's happened."

I rolled my head to the side, then leaned forward, whispered, "He wants to capture the dolphins. Not save them."

"Okay," Chris said. "There's no doubt in my mind that there is more to *that* story. Which I'm sure I'll learn at some point. But something else has happened. Obviously. Tell me what."

I huffed. "So, you're a psychologist now, that it? I knew you were thinking about a new career."

"Does it have anything to do with this ex-wife?"

"What? No."

"Not even a little?"

"I talked to her. And…"

"And?"

"And I like her. She's sweet. I mean, I wanted to dislike

her, you know. But I can't. She's kind and all that, even though…"

Chris's eyebrows raised. "Even though…?"

"Even though she cheated on him."

Chris sat back. "Shut up."

"Told me herself."

"Oh, that man…"

"If she hadn't, they'd be living in Montana right now, in a cute little house with a couple of kids and…"

Chris gave me a strange look. "You say that like it's a death sentence."

"Yeah, well…" My drink arrived. I sucked down half of it.

Chris took it from my hand, set it on the table in front of me. "Yep, this has gotten out of hand."

"Out of hand is right. He said he loved me. Ha! Lovvvvvve. Can you believe that?"

"Love!" Chris sat back, shook his head. "I knew it had to be something serious. Yes, this is definitely a problem."

"Don't make fun of me."

"Okay, back up the truck. Start at the beginning."

I reached for my drink, downed the rest of the glass.

"Hurry up and talk before that rum gets to your head."

"We were talking about love. Actually, we were talking about his ex wife. You know, how she cheated on him. And he said you have to let go, be vulnerable, something like that." I leaned in again. "The next thing I know, he's listing all these things about me, my pink cheeks, my sassy personality, then bam, right out of left field, he says he loves me."

Chris stared at me, waiting. "And?"

"And I…I stuttered a lot. I started picturing the little house, the kids, dirty diapers. I swear, I was hyperventilating."

"No doubt."

"I mean, Chris. Can you see me in an apron?"

"No dear, you don't have a domestic bone in your body, but—"

"I saw this white picket fence, and it was closing in on me, like in the movies, you know, those horror films, where you're paralyzed and stuff gets all out of shape."

"Okay, so the rum is kicking in."

"I mean, you gotta be a grown up yourself, you know."

"Yeah?"

"You should've seen him, with those eyes. And that chest. I mean, you know Dalton. God, he's so…"

"Um, yeah."

"And I'm standing there like a dope, stuttering away. And he's going on about how everything will work out, we can conquer anything." My head felt a little dizzy. "He said he knows I love him too, to just say it. And then I realized what we need to do to save the dolphins."

"Wait? What? So you didn't respond? You didn't say you loved him back?"

"I said…I mean, it all happened so fast. The dolphins popped into my mind, how they're tethered, you know, tied down, and I said, hey, we can help them escape and—"

"So, you changed the subject?"

"Well, no, I mean, yes. I guess." I clamped my hands into fists. "You know how my brain works."

He had that deadpan look. "Yeah, like a jigsaw puzzle in a blender."

"I know, right?"

"What the hell is wrong with you?"

I sighed. "I know."

"So, then what happened?"

"He left."

"Oh, man." He thought for a bit. "Okay. This is Dalton. He's not going to go all nut job on us. He knows you're a…you're you."

"Now he's on a mission to capture those innocent dolphins. In the name of naval security. Just to spite me."

He looked me in the eyes. "Do you really think that?"

I turned away. "No."

"So, what are you going to do?"

I raised my hand, gestured for the waitress, pointed at my empty glass. "Have another Bahama Mama. That was damn good."

"Poppy, what are you going to do?"

I looked down at the ball of yarn. "Maybe you could teach me to knit."

"Oh, great."

I bit down hard on my lip. "Well, I can't let them capture those dolphins."

"Get yourself together, girl. I mean about Dalton."

I shrugged.

"Oh my god, you're hopeless."

"Don't say that."

"You're pathetic, you know that. It's so obvious what's happening here. You're scared because you know you love him too, but you don't want to get hurt. So you're—I don't even know what. This is cause for an intervention."

"Don't be ridiculous. I'm scared because—"

"I've read about people who do this. Self sabotage. It's not that uncommon. Wait, what'd you say?"

"What'd I say when?"

"Just now. You said you're scared because and then you didn't finish."

"I'm not scared of anything. I'm rough and tough and I'm going to kick some ass." The rum was making me feel warm, relaxed. I could think now. "First, I need to get the trackers off their feet, I mean fins."

"Oh, here we go," Chris said.

"No, I'm serious. I need my own plan."

"Oh, I know. Next you're going to ask me to—"

"And I need your help."

CHAPTER 16

"We have to get the trackers off. How do we do that? How do we get them to come close enough to do that? How do they come off?"

Kerrie and Natalie stared at me, trying to follow my barrage of questions. The three cups of coffee Chris had poured down my throat brought me some clarity, and I was on a mission.

"Where's your partner?" Kerrie said, looking past me. "The good-looking guy who—"

"Yeah, he's running down another side to this."

She looked confused. "Another side?"

"Forget it. Chris here is going to assist for now."

She sat back, her eyebrows knit with concern.

"I don't mean to be curt. Just, time's a wastin' you know."

"What did your supervisor say?"

"Can't call out. The storm. But we don't have time to wait. The trackers. How do we get them off?"

"Okay. Um." Kerrie glanced at Natalie. "Why do you need to remove the trackers?"

This wasn't going as I'd planned. "What's the problem?" I asked. My head throbbed like a tiny wrecking ball was banging against my temple from the inside. *Note to self: coffee then rum then coffee equals not good.*

"The science we'd glean," Natalie said, "from learning about how these dolphins, once captive, will adapt to being back in the wild would be—"

"Unprecedented," Kerrie said.

"You mean if the dolphins stay here," I said.

"Wherever they decide to go. That's the point. We want the GPS information."

Natalie looked hopeful. "Can't you get the government to help with that?"

"I wish I had those kind of resources. Even if I did, the time it would take—doesn't matter. I'm concerned about the lives of these dolphins *right now*. I want those trackers off so they have a chance. So they can't be found and recaptured."

"You're right, of course," Kerrie said. "You're right."

Good. "Besides, they'll probably decide to stay here."

"Maybe," Natalie said.

I locked onto Kerrie again. "So how do we remove the trackers?"

"Well, the trackers are bolted to the dorsal fin."

"Bolted?"

"Yeah. Like an ear piercing. But a larger bolt."

"Can I unscrew the bolt by hand?"

"I don't know. Most are designed to fall off after a certain time. But these—I don't know."

"What's the worst case scenario?"

Her eyes traveled around the table as she thought. "That you'd have to rip the fin. Which the dolphin would survive. They are highly resilient. But it hurts, for sure."

"What about bolt cutters?"

"You wouldn't be able to get the cutter between the fin and the nut. You'd be better to unscrew the bolts. If the dolphin will let you. You'll need a wrench, or what do you call those—?"

"Pliers?" Natalie offered.

"Yeah, two. We have some."

Chris asked, "Couldn't you just break off the antennas?"

I turned to Kerrie.

"Maybe," she said. "But—" She bit her lip.

"What is it?"

"Either way, what happens when they realize they've been tampered with? They'll know something is up. They'll know we're messing with them."

"They don't get the satellite info instantly, right? The storm could be interfering with transmissions, right? So they wouldn't make that assumption immediately."

"Yeah, okay, but what about when they see the dolphins and notice that the trackers are gone?"

"The dolphins don't have any reason to go back to their boat, right? You said they're feeding themselves, that they're doing fine in the wild."

She shrugged. "We think so, but—"

"Okay. This is their chance. We have to help them get free. Let's do this."

Kerrie didn't move. She and Natalie exchanged a look of concern.

"What?" I asked.

"You're making a big assumption."

"And what's that?"

They glanced at each other again. Kerrie said, "That you could find them."

"Okay. Maybe I can't. But surely you know how to find them?"

She shook her head. "It doesn't work that way. We go days without seeing the resident dolphins. We just don't know that much about them."

"Well, you must have some idea. I mean, where have you seen them so far? Has it been around the same area?"

Resigned, she said, "Well, after the storm passes, maybe—"

"No, we don't have time. We can't wait. Where would they go during the storm?"

Kerrie's eyes grew wide and she shook her head. "I have no

idea. We don't even know where ours go at night. During a storm, I just don't know."

"Take your best guess."

Natalie chimed in. "We think they head out to deep water. But if so, you'll never find them. It would be like a needle in a haystack. But…"

"But what?"

"But if these dolphins have been trained, they might have been trained for this kind of scenario, too. I don't know. Maybe they'd go where their trainers' boat would go. In that case, maybe they'd head for the lee of the island?"

"All right. That's where we'll start. We need a boat."

Kerrie stared at me. "Wish I had one. We always go with the dive shop on their boat. But we can't—"

"That's the boat we'll take then. Chris can drive."

"Just the two of you? Out in this storm? Are you crazy?"

"I'll go," said Natalie.

Kerrie gave Natalie a sharp, motherly look. "Like I said, there's a storm. A big one."

"All the better," I said. "No one will be out there to see us."

Eight foot swells in a small dive boat… Yeah. No problem. Poor Chris. I shouldn't have brought him.

Wind whipped spray off the tops of the waves that instantly mixed with the rain and slapped us in our faces.

Six inches of water sloshed around in the bottom of the boat.

Natalie pointed. "I think I see them!"

"Great," Chris said, the word laced with sarcasm. He'd been looking a little green and lobbying to head back for the dock.

"Head that way," I told him.

"Aye, aye, Captain!"

"How do we get them to come up to the boat?" I asked

Natalie.

She shrugged. "I don't know. I have no idea what their whistle calls are. They've been coming on their own."

I grabbed a handful of the frozen shrimp we'd bought at the grocery store and, as soon as we got close, I tossed it into the water.

One of the dolphins zipped toward it.

"Yeah, you want some more?" I tossed another handful into the water. "I think they like the shrimp."

The boat rolled up on a wave, then surfed down the other side. I lost sight of the dolphin.

"Stay with them," I told Chris.

"Are you kidding? It's all I've got to keep us from rolling over." He had a life vest on and an orange PFD strapped around his waist.

The dolphin popped back up alongside the boat. "Toss some more shrimp," I told Natalie. "I'll get the pliers."

The boat surged up a wave, then down the other side.

"Keep it steady!" I hollered to Chris.

He gave me a sarcastic thumbs up.

"If I toss them one at a time, I think he might stay alongside the boat. What do you think?" Natalie said.

"Do it."

I flipped my leg over the side of the boat, straddling the gunwale, with the pliers in my hands. Rain pelted me in the face.

"You're nuts, you know that!" Chris shouted.

"Just keep it steady."

The dolphin popped up, grabbed a shrimp and was gone again.

"I'm not sure that will work," I said.

"Maybe it would be easier if you get them to bow ride," Natalie said.

"What do you mean?"

"They love to ride the wave pushed from the bow as the boat plows through the water. It's fun."

"Of course it is," Chris muttered.

"I don't know if they'll do it in the big waves."

"Well, it's worth a try. What do we do?"

"Keep it steady. Try staying in the trough so it's smooth."

Chris turned the boat.

"Five to eight miles an hour is fast enough. And if we head back toward shore, maybe they'll follow us into calmer water."

"Good idea," Chris said.

Two dolphins emerged alongside the boat. "There's two," I shouted.

"Give 'em a minute. They might do it."

They disappeared below the surface, then popped up together, side by side, right at the bow of the boat. "Yes!"

I lay down on my belly, clamping onto the gunwale with my thighs, reaching with the pliers. The dolphins pumped their peduncles, their flukes moving up and down, to keep up with the boat. They dipped under and up again so fast, there was no way I would be able to get a hold of the tracker. Even if I did, it would rip off, tearing the fin as they dove again.

"They're moving around too much," I said.

Natalie leaned over me. "I don't know what else to do."

"I need to get into the water with them."

"In these waves?" She and Chris both shook their heads.

"Below the surface, it's calm. If I can get them to follow me to the bottom, maybe they'll slow and I can get close."

"That's a big maybe," Natalie said, hanging onto the handrail with both hands, her hair whipping around her face.

All the SCUBA gear I needed was on board. Tanks, BCs, weights, fins, and masks. I picked up a BC.

"Oh, no. Not a good idea." Chris shook his head at me. "First of all, you're not supposed to dive alone. Second, how are we going to get you off this boat? Let alone back into it. Third—"

"I'll swim to shore."

"Are you nuts?"

"Dalton did it last night."

"Dalton's a trained SEAL."

With my feet wide apart to keep me steady, I bent over and buckled the BC to a tank. "I'm doing this."

Natalie helped me with fins and a mask. "For the record," she said, "I don't think it's a good idea either."

"Noted," I said. "Just head back to the dock."

Natalie looked at Chris. He shook his head. He knew there was nothing he could say to stop me.

"Give me the bag of shrimp," I said and spit in my mask.

With the air cranked on, everything strapped to my back, mask in place, Natalie handed me the shrimp and I plunged over the side.

Bubbles surrounded me as I submerged.

The storm had churned the sea, stirring up debris. The visibility was bad, maybe twenty feet.

As I sank, the frenzy of the waves subsided, and I settled on the sandy bottom. The only sound was my breathing—whoosh, whoosh, whoosh.

Right away, one of the tagged dolphins appeared out of the abyss, curious.

I pushed shrimp from the bag and he dipped, grabbing it in his mouth, then was gone again, without the slightest movement of his tail.

Now, come closer. I held out a shrimp. The dolphin zoomed in from behind me and snatched it from my hand.

Crap. That's not going to work.

I needed the dolphin to hold steady, the dorsal fin facing my way. Or rest on the bottom. Something. How in the world was I going to do that?

The dolphin circled above me, dashing in and out of the bubbles emitted from my regulator as I exhaled.

Stop playing. This is serious. I need you down here, at the bottom with me.

What had Kerrie said about crater feeding? Something about using their rostrums to poke around at the bottom, searching under the sand?

Could that work? I took out another shrimp, waved it around, and shoved it into the sand under my fin.

The dolphin swiveled past, chirping away. Then he paused, nose down, nudging my fin, his dorsal fin within reach.

I raised the pliers, and he bucked, knocking them from my hands, and zipped away.

I dropped to my knees and felt around in the sand. My hand locked on to one pair. Where was the other? It had to be right here. Or had he knocked it farther away then I'd thought?

My hand grasped onto something. *Whew. Found 'em!*

I gripped the two pair of pliers in my hands and held them up like a cowboy brandishing two six-shooters. *C'mon, now. I'm ready for you.*

The dolphin came back, dipped downward, poking in the sand and exposing the fin. I grabbed ahold of the tracker with one hand and with the other, I clamped the pliers down on the nut, then the other pliers on the other end of the bolt. Two turns and it broke off. *Got it!*

The tracker fell to the ocean floor. *Yes!* I picked it up and stuffed it inside my zippered pocket. *One down. Four to go.*

The dolphin spun around me, chirping and rolling. I couldn't be sure, but he seemed gleeful, as if he knew I'd helped him somehow.

Now tell your friends. I'm not going to hurt you. I'm here to help.

Moments later, another appeared. I waved another shrimp in front of me, then tucked it into the sand below my fin. This dolphin came right to me, flipped his tail up, and moved next to me, as if to offer his fin. Was he—? Did he know? It was as though he was asking for me to take off the tracker.

I quickly broke it free.

The dolphin dipped and spun. I couldn't believe it. They knew. They wanted them off!

Soon, two more appeared. These two were more tentative. They darted past, then on a second pass, slowed, looking me over. I tried my trick once more, waving shrimp around for them to see, then tucked them under my fins. They turned and disappeared into the murky sea, beyond my vision.

C'mon back now. It won't hurt, I swear.

The first dolphin swooped in and tried to pick off the shrimp. *Not you!* I held my foot firm, keeping the shrimp buried. The dolphin flipped his tail and spun in a vertical loop, clicking and chirping. Was he frustrated?

The two with trackers still attached appeared again, low across the sand, incoming, like a couple of torpedoes. I wasn't sure if they were going to plow me over. Full-speed they came, then right before me, they dropped their rostrums to the sand and hovered, inches from me.

I grabbed one by the tracker and twisted the nut. Then the other. And their trackers were off.

I let out a yelp of glee that muffled through my regulator.

Now, I had one more. The fifth dolphin. The one causing trouble for the Russians. The one that likely led the escape. The one they'd kill if she didn't cooperate.

I hadn't seen any sign of her.

Generally, I didn't like to anthropomorphize, but I assumed she was female. She had to be. Strong-willed, unwilling to follow orders, free-spirited, determined to escape. Yep, she and I had a connection. A bond. I had to help her. I had to get that tracker off. But she was nowhere around.

I dropped more shrimp, trying to lure her in if she was

nearby, but the others darted in and scarfed them up.

C'mon, girl. The others get it. Where are you?

Then, on the edge of visibility, a shadow swam by. Was it her? The shape…was that a shark? Tiger shark? A shot of adrenaline zipped through my veins. I didn't want to see a tiger shark. Not now. Not ever, really.

But no, this shadow didn't move like a shark. It was definitely a dolphin.

My breathing returned to normal.

Silly, Poppy. There was no reason to fear a shark, out here, in its normal habitat. But sometimes, no amount of logic steels the nerves. Besides, I was surrounded by dolphins. There are endless stories of dolphins protecting humans from sharks, all over the world.

The four dolphins circled, their attention on me, as playful as ever.

The fifth dolphin stayed at a distance, circling, where I caught only momentary glimpses.

Then, in a synchronized move, the other four dolphins turned away and disappeared into the deep blue.

What happened? Where'd they go?

My tank was running low on air. 500psi. I had to head to the surface and to shore.

I'd have to come back out and try again to get the fifth one.

When I popped up at the surface, *Droppin' Skirts* idled nearby, rolling in the surf. When they spotted me, Mike brought the boat around. Tom threw a line for me to grab and dragged me toward the boat.

He lay on his stomach on the swim platform on the back of the boat, holding on with one hand. The platform slammed into the water, then raised five feet into the air on a wave. I would have to time it just right, or the platform would come down on top of me.

"Keep it steady!" he yelled to Mike at the helm. To me he

said, "Stay to the side. Don't get under it."

"Roger that."

First, I took off my gear and shoved it toward him. As the stern came down, he grabbed hold of it. He didn't have to lift. He held on as the boat went up a wave, then set it down as the platform dropped again, all in one motion.

"I'm going to have to grab you. You'll have to come up the rope, close enough, at just the right time."

"Okay," I said.

The platform slammed down next to me, but I missed my chance.

"Take your time," Tom said. "I'm ready for you." He held out his hands.

The boat rode up again and, hand over hand, I pulled myself close. As the platform smacked the water, Tom's arms were around me, and I was lifted into the air. He rolled and I rolled with him. I scrambled to my knees and grabbed hold of the swim handle.

"Gotcha!"

We both got to our feet and duck-walked to the seats.

"What are you doing out here?" I asked once I'd got my balance.

Mike handed me a glass of water. "We saw you leave the marina in the dive boat, figured you might need some help. Your friend Chris was relieved to see us, by the way. It was the only reason he went on back to the marina. Poor guy looked a little green."

"Yeah, but I thought you were on Dalton's side."

"We're all on one team," Tom said with a fatherly tone.

I pulled the trackers from the BC pocket and held them out for them to see. "I removed their trackers. Four of them. The fifth wouldn't come close enough for me to get it. Then they all disappeared, as if—"

Tom sighed. "Yeah, we kinda figured."

"What? How'd you know?"

"We've had the hydrophone in the water. We recorded a high frequency sound. Possibly a signal."

"You mean—?"

"Yeah. We think the Russians are communicating with them using underwater sound amplification."

I looked to Mike, then back to Tom. "So, they're not using whistles?" I knew it was stating the obvious. Somehow, I was two steps behind.

Tom was shaking his head. "This way, they can give the dolphins commands from a long distance away."

"So, the trackers being off—"

"Doesn't matter. They don't need to find them. They can call them home like dogs."

"Dammit!"

CHAPTER 17

Once we got back in the bay and had the boat tied back up at the dock, I turned to the guys and asked, "You don't really think Hyland is going to want us to help kidnap the dolphins?"

Tom stared at me.

Mike looked away, chewing on his thumbnail.

C'mon, guys.

Tom finally said, "You know, Dalton, he—"

"Don't tell me you're afraid of Dalton?"

"Listen," Tom said, placing his hands on my forearms and looking into my eyes. "We know enough to know that we are too far down the food chain to make decisions on our own."

Hot frustration traveled up my neck.

"We follow orders," he went on. "And, right now, we don't have new orders."

"Yeah, but—"

"But nothing," Mike said, digging something out of his ear. "I'm already on shaky ground as it is."

That was true. He'd damn near got us killed on the last op.

"And so are you," he added.

My jaw tightened. "I'm not the one who—"

"All right." Tom held up his hands as he stepped between us. "The point is, it doesn't matter what we think. We don't act without direction."

"I don't believe that," I said. I wanted to slap them both.

"This is an elite team. Not because we have exhaustive training like Navy SEALs. It's because we're smart. We know how to get to the heart of an operation and expose criminal activity. And we do it all for the good of the animals. In this situation, we know exactly what to do." I threw up my hands. "But hey, if you want to wait for *Mom* to give you a permission slip, you go right ahead."

I found Chris and Natalie at the dive dock, watching for me.

"There you are!" Chris shouted when he saw me, relieved.

"Tom and Mike picked me up."

We moved to the leeward side of the building, under a slatted roof out of the rain. I told them about the acoustical summons and the dolphins disappearing.

"So, it was all for nothing?" Natalie asked.

I shook my head. I had an idea.

"Oh-kay?" Chris moaned.

"I know what we need to do. The question is, are you up for it?"

"Oh god," Chris said.

"Up for what?" Natalie asked.

"These guys think I'm an intern. An animal lover. I've got red hair, so, I'm hot-headed, right?"

Chris nodded. "Um, yeah, you're saying that like it's a ridiculous stereotype but—"

"Fine, what do young, idealistic, passionate dolphin-lovers do when they see dolphins being harmed?"

Chris groaned. "Here it comes."

"I can tell you what the Sea Shepherds do to whalers."

Natalie nodded. She was getting the idea.

"Butyric acid. Methylcellulose. Prop fouling."

Chris backed away, his hands up. "Acid? You can't be serious."

"Butyric acid," I said. "A homemade stink bomb. It smells like vomit."

His lips curled up.

"We use the cover to get close to their boat and we destroy that damn acoustic device."

"Yes!" Natalie said, then immediately lost her enthusiasm. "But getting a hold of some butyric acid and methylcellulose on this island—you can't even get decent chocolate."

"Right," I said. "Well, I think—"

"What does Dalton say about it?" Chris asked.

"Doesn't matter."

"But doesn't Dalton—"

"I don't need Dalton's approval."

"Okay." He backed away.

"I don't need Dalton and I don't need to call my boss, which I can't do now with the storm anyway. I'm calling the shots here."

"Okay," Chris said, his voice gone soft.

"We have to give these dolphins a fighting chance to get away."

"Right on," Natalie said.

I turned to her. "We need the feces of an ungulate. One with the stomach—what do you call that?—you know, where the food ferments in the stomach. Horses? Cattle? Are there any on the island?"

She shook her head.

"What about a goat?"

"I think there is one goat, on the North Island."

"Good. And okra has a high concentration of methyl cellulose. Do you know—"

"Yes, yes. We can get okra. Frozen. But it's commonly served here on the island."

"Vegetables?" Chris said. "Are you kidding?"

"Methyl cellulose is slippery. Makes it hard to walk on the

deck of a boat."

"Ah."

"Remember, it's all a façade anyway."

"Right."

"We just need a way to get it and the stink bombs onto their deck. The Shepherds throw glass bottles that break on the steel ships. But in this situation, I don't think we could—"

"I know." Natalie grinned with devilish intent. "How about a water balloon launcher, with biodegradable balloons, no less."

I smiled. "Now we're talking."

While Chris shopped for okra and Natalie, having drawn the short straw, collected goat droppings, I ran another errand. To the Bimini Big Game Club.

The pool area was deserted. Palm trees whipped in the wind and rain showered the patio. I ducked into the Bar & Grill. Rod and Alison sat at a corner table watching the television and sharing a fried shrimp appetizer.

"I'm so sorry to interrupt," I said. "I just have a quick question."

Rod shot up from his chair and pulled one out for me.

"No need," I said. "Like I said, quick question."

"Sure. Happy to help." He eased back into the chair next to Alison.

"The boat, with the Russians. You mentioned there was communication equipment on board. But did you see any audio equipment? Anything that would *produce* sounds underwater?"

"You mean like a diver recall transducer?"

"Um, *maybe*?"

"You're wondering if they had an output actuator?"

"Well, I don't know what it's called, but—"

"An underwater loudspeaker. Yes, that equipment was on board."

I tried to hide my excitement. "Okay, what did it look like?"

He stood back up. "Is Dalton thinking of going back out there? Because I can be ready in—"

"No, no." I held up my hands as if to block him. "I just need to know that I could identify it. If the opportunity arises." *And it will.* "I need to know what I'm looking for."

"Oh." He didn't seem convinced. "Well, they're simple, actually. A speaker or I think that one had several speakers on one cord." He cupped his hands, holding them about ten inches apart. "About the size of a pie plate. When in use, it would be deployed over the side, into the water, and likely have a line attached with a weight on the bottom to keep it submerged."

"And you're sure you saw one? That kind, I mean?"

He nodded. "Affirmative."

Two hours later, Chris, Natalie, and I were back at my room. Okra bubbled in a pot on the hotplate. Outside my door, the goat dung steeped in the juices at the bottom of a trash barrel.

"As soon as the okra mash cools, we'll fill the balloons. We can start with the goat dung."

Chris shook his head. "That's where I draw the line."

"C'mon."

"Nope. No way."

"Fine," I said.

Natalie and I tied bandanas over our noses. "How bad can it be?"

She'd brought an old ladle and a funnel.

Holding our breath, we filled one balloon at a time.

"Omigod," Natalie said, trying not to retch. "That is nasty."

"That's the point." I held my breath to keep from gagging. "Let's just get it done."

Soon, we had twenty-five balloons filled.

The okra mash filled up another fifteen.

We carefully loaded them into a hard-sided cooler.

"This is a great start," I said. "They won't mistake the message anyway."

Once Chris and Natalie left for the night, I slumped down in the chair. What an exhausting day.

What was Dalton up to?

Thoughts of his kisses warmed my insides. *Maybe I should go find him.*

But we'd just argue. What was going on with him? I'd never seen him so worked up.

Yeah, I needed to go find him.

I grabbed my raincoat and put it on as I went out the door.

He'd been given a room on the second floor of a house two streets over. It had an outside entrance. When I got there, no lights were on. It was only eight thirty.

Where might he be?

I walked down on the dock. Lights were on in *Droppin' Skirts*. Mike and Tom were sitting in the salon, but not Dalton. I went back down the dock.

Gaspar's Revenge was no longer docked. Jesse probably had it anchored out in the bay. If Dalton was with him, I would have to find a dinghy and drive around in the dark.

No. *Let it go.* If he wanted to see me, he would.

On my way back to my room, I went by his place again, but the room was still dark.

I needed to get some sleep anyway. Tomorrow was going to be a big day.

CHAPTER 18

The rain had stopped overnight and blue sky cut through above, but the ocean was still a maelstrom of big waves. Chris and I waited at the water sports shack, sipping our coffee, until finally, at 9:15, an older Bahamian man ambled in. His hair was as white as snow and his ebony skin as weathered and wrinkled as old leather. He sat in the well-worn chair, and when he smiled, there was a wide gap between his middle teeth.

"Can I help yuh, miss?" he asked, his voice like an old island song.

"I'd like to rent a WaveRunner," I said.

"Ah, sorry, miss, can't do dat," he said, shaking his head. "Not during dis blow."

I pulled out my government Amex card and handed it to him. "How about if I pay for three, but just take one?"

He shrugged, then looked at the card and smiled. "Well den, kick up rumpus, miss," he said, running my card and handing it back, along with the key.

Chris and I headed for the dock where Natalie met us with the cooler. We strapped our makeshift stink bomb case onto the back of the WaveRunner, buckled our life vests, and climbed aboard.

Chris had agreed to drive while I sat on the back and deployed the bombs, but the balloon launcher was a huge slingshot apparatus that, we found, wasn't going to work on a WaveRunner; it'd be really difficult to aim. We'd have to throw our homemade balloon-bombs by hand. Since Chris had a much better throwing arm, a fact that I had a hard time admitting, we switched seats.

"Good luck," Natalie said and waved as we left the harbor.

As we turned out of the bay, headed for open ocean and big waves, I slowed.

"Chris. Thanks for doing this," I said.

"It'll be fun," he replied with a grin.

"No, I mean, being here. Everything."

"Yeah." He nodded. "What are friends for? Let's just get this speaker thing. Then we can work on the real problem. You and Dalton."

"You never let up."

"Nope. And by the way, take it easy. Don't kill me out there. We both know you're a crazy driver."

I gave him a grin back, said, "Hang on," and squeezed the throttle. We shot through the water, hit a wave straight on, and launched into the air.

Chris let out a squeal.

We hit a second wave and went airborne again, this time slamming down so hard it knocked us forward. Water sprayed over our heads.

"What'd I say?" he shouted. "Slow it down!"

"Roger that," I said, and took the next wave with a little less throttle.

We rounded the island and headed north to the area we guessed they'd most likely be. Each wave sent us skyward, then plunging down the trough in a steady rhythm.

What seemed like twenty minutes later, we spotted their vessel. For whatever reason, they hadn't chosen to take cover from the storm in the lee of the island. Or maybe they had and they were already back out. Whichever, they wouldn't be here much longer. Not if I had anything to do with it.

I drove straight for them. There was no point in trying to be stealthy about it. I wanted them to see it was me, not Kerrie or Natalie. Me, the intern. With the red hair. They could threaten me all they wanted. I wasn't going to tolerate them harming these dolphins.

As I approached the boat, two men stood at the stern, watching. One held a pair of binoculars to his eyes. Then I spotted in the water, behind the boat, four dolphins.

I drove the WaveRunner straight at them. The dolphins would dive out of the way. Once I was within range, I said to Chris, "As we pass, fire at will!"

A balloon shot through the air and hit the stern, right in the center, and exploded on contact. Liquid goat shit sprayed everywhere.

Chris let out a whoop.

The men jumped back, then the odor hit them and their hands raised to cover their noses.

"Take that!" I yelled as I spun the WaveRunner around to make another pass.

Chris launched another, then another.

I circled back. "Hit 'em with the slippery stuff."

Two more balloons fired into the air, one then the other. Only one hit. Splat.

The men disappeared inside the boat.

"Keep hitting 'em," I told Chris. "We need to come around for our prize."

I could see the audio device, hanging from a cleat on the starboard side.

"Oh man, oh man," Chris yelped.

"What?" Then the smell hit me.

"One broke open in the cooler."

I slowed. "Rinse it out. Hurry."

My throat involuntarily constricted.

A shot rang out. A gunshot.

"They're shooting at us?" I said in disbelief. *At animal rights kids?*

"Omigod!" Chris shouted. "Go, go, go!"

I squeezed the throttle and shot over a wave. We slammed down the other side.

Shots zinged by and—smack—a bullet hit the engine cover.

I kept the hammer down. "Hang on!" I shouted to Chris.

Up and over another wave we went, then another.

What the hell! They shot at us? Of all the scenarios I considered, I hadn't thought they'd shoot at us. They were *shooting* at us!

We slammed into a wave too hard and Chris fell sideways and slid off the WaveRunner.

I rammed the handlebars to the left, the nose dipped, and the ass end spun around. He bobbed in the surf.

"Get on!"

His arms flailed at air. I grabbed his hand and hauled him back aboard, knocking the cooler off the back.

Another shot rang out and the back panel shattered to pieces.

I hit the gas.

We raced toward the marina, Chris latched onto me, his arms locked around my waist.

"What the hell? They shot at us," he hollered in my ear.

I shook my head. It didn't make sense. They were in foreign waters, illegally harassing dolphins. Keeping a low profile would be their best approach. But to shoot at us?

Had our time run out? Were they shooting the fifth dolphin? And they figured they were bugging out anyway, get me out of their hair?

"I need to get you back to the marina." I had to get that audio device, no matter what. It was now or never.

"Well, yeah—wait. You're not gonna—we didn't get the speaker thing, so you're gonna—oh, no. You're not going back out there?"

"I have to. It's the only way those dolphins will have a chance to escape."

"Poppy, they were *shooting* at us. With guns. Real ones." He pointed at the engine cover, barely still attached to the front end of the WaveRunner. "See."

"Yeah, but—"

"But nothing!"

"They shot a few warning shots at us." It might've been true.

"Warning shots! That one parted my hair."

"That's why I'll go alone this time."

"You're certifiable. It's official. You've lost your mind. I'm hosting an intervention. Seriously."

"Don't worry, they won't really shoot me." *I hope.*

"Are you kidding me right now? Because sometimes you kid and I can't tell."

"The attention a murder would bring would end their stay here in The Bahamas in a big way. They can't be that stupid."

"Sure they can! Or that ruthless. They're Russians."

"They were trying to scare us. That was all."

"Poppy, you—"

I gave him the look.

He held his hands up. "Okay. I know that look. When you get those crazy eyes. I'll be at the Hilton. Emptying my drawers."

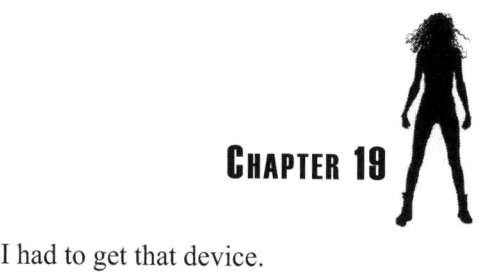

CHAPTER 19

I had to get that device.

My plan—go straight at the boat. They wouldn't expect me to do that again. All I had to do was grab a hold of the cord, wrap it around the handle bar on the WaveRunner, and drive away. One pass. That was it.

At least then the dolphins would have a fighting chance.

The clouds had gone completely and the warm sun turned the water a turquoise blue, but the waves still rolled in from the southwest.

I headed right back in the direction where the boat had been, but as I approached, it was gone. Gone.

I looked around. They couldn't have gone far. But which way?

To the north, I thought I saw a boat. But then it disappeared again.

There it was again.

I clamped down on the throttle and headed toward it.

I wasn't stopping until I had that cord in my hands.

With every wave, water splashed over the front of the WaveRunner. I kept it up. Maybe they wouldn't hear me coming and I wouldn't have to dodge bullets at all.

Maybe this was crazy. Maybe I was losing my mind. Who does this, anyway? Ride straight toward a loaded gun? Not someone with responsibility. Not someone who has someone counting on them. Like Alison. She'd never do something like this. And Rod, he shouldn't either. Not with a baby on the way.

No. It was people like me. Crazy, irresponsible nut jobs.

Well, whatever. It was who I was and I was doing it. I was going to get that damn speaker from those Russians, no matter what I had to do.

The boat came into view. The starboard side. I needed to get along the starboard side.

The boat was moving. Someone was at the helm. Good. That meant only one of them was free to shoot at me.

But was the speaker still in the water? Damn. If they were under way, they'd have pulled it up.

As I got closer, I could see it flopping in the water on the side of the boat. They'd forgotten it. *Yes!*

Unless…? The dolphins were following them.

Did that mean…? Was the fifth dolphin with them? Or had they killed her? Or maybe they'd decided to leave without her after I'd gone after them and caused trouble?

I couldn't think about that now. *Concentrate.* My hands gripped the handles tighter.

I'd have to bring the WaveRunner up alongside the boat, match their speed, and grab the cord. But in these waves, that would be a feat.

And that was only if whomever was at the helm held a steady course for me. And I didn't get shot.

I needed another plan.

But what?

Kaboom! A gunshot.

I zigged left, then right.

Yep, I was crazy. Who could possibly want to have a relationship with a risk-taking, adrenaline junkie like me?

Dalton would kill me if he knew what I was up to.

I kept my hand on the throttle as I ducked low, full speed ahead.

Just get the speaker.

The boat was no more than a hundred and fifty yards away. Another shot ricocheted across the water. This guy wasn't kidding.

A hundred yards.

I aimed for the starboard side.

Fifty yards.

The man was shouting. Angry words. What was he saying? I had no idea. I speak five languages, but Russian wasn't one of them.

Twenty yards. The cord was hanging there. Almost in reach.

Full throttle. Within inches, I threw my weight to the side and rammed the WaveRunner into the hull of the boat. Fiberglass connected with the steel hull in a shattering crunch.

The boat slowed. More angry Russian words came at me.

My WaveRunner righted itself. I reached for the cord, grabbed hold, wrapped it around the handle, and squeezed the throttle.

Nothing happened.

The WaveRunner had stalled.

Dammit!

I glanced back. A weapon was aimed at me.

"Hands up!" The man shouted. My stalker.

"What? Are you gonna arrest me?" I shouted back.

With a flick of my wrist, I turned the key off, then on again, flipped the switch, and… nothing. *Shit.* The stalker still had his gun trained on me but didn't shoot. Before I could sort out why, I felt his hands at the top of my head, grabbing me by the hair.

"What the hell, man!" It hurt like a bitch.

"You stupid girl," he said in a thick Russian accent.

Girl?!

He was leaning over the rail, clamping down harder on my

hair, shaking my head.

I stood up on the WaveRunner, reached up and clamped my right hand onto his wrist to relieve the pain at my scalp.

Nausea brewed in my stomach and I struggled to keep from vomiting. It was the stench from my own stink bomb. *Irony*.

You're an activist, Poppy, a spoiled, little, impulsive activist.

"You monster!" I yelled, startling him. "You're harassing these dolphins when they just want to live in peace and play and be happy and you're destroying their lives!" I let my knees go slack and racked my body with fake sobs.

He held onto my hair, but seemed unsure what to do next. Men... They get unreasonably uncomfortable when a woman starts crying.

"Who sent you?" he finally said, his voice stern.

"Let me go," I wailed.

"Enough," he said, yanking my head back so I was facing him. "Now you calm down."

Damn, that hurt.

He shoved the pistol in my face. "You tell me truth."

I stared back at him.

"You have five seconds."

Something in his eyes told me he wasn't bluffing. He could shoot me right here, right now. No one would see him. They'd be back in Cuba before anyone even missed me. I had to act fast.

I grabbed his elbow with my other hand and let my knees collapse, pulling him over the side with me. On the way down, I rammed the heel of my hand into the side of his head. He hit the dash of the WaveRunner with a thud, then slumped over and slid into the water.

"Now start, you son of a bitch," I said to the WaveRunner. I turned the key on and flipped the switch. It rumbled to life. "Houston, we have lift-off!"

The cord was still wrapped around the handle. I clamped down on the throttle and the WaveRunner shot up a wave and away from the boat, the speaker flopping behind me.

I reached out behind me and flipped my middle finger in the air. *Call me a girl one more time!* Immature, I know, but it felt like the thing a pissed off activist would do.

Who was I kidding? I'd royally messed this one up. No doubt I'd blown my cover. I closed my eyes and took a couple deep breaths to calm myself and catch my bearings. I probably should have done more yoga on the trip. Maybe I would have been able to better control my impulses—with this mission, with Dalton.

I headed for shore, but I didn't get far from the boat when the engine started to sputter and died.

Crap!

Turning the key again didn't help. Nothing.

I looked back. The Russians hadn't bothered to follow me. If they knew I had the sound amplifier, they didn't care and after my little escape moves, they probably decided I was more trouble than I was worth.

The back end of the WaveRunner started to dip. It was sinking. I leaned to the side to take a look. Swiss cheese. *Oops.*

It tilted backward even more and the entire back end sunk under water.

Shore was at least two miles away. I'd have to swim. Thankfully, I had a life jacket on. But the waves weren't rolling in that direction.

The nose of the WaveRunner was the only part above water now. It'd be on the bottom within minutes. Hyland wasn't going to be happy when she got the bill.

I abandoned it, oriented myself toward shore, and started kicking my feet. This was going to be a long afternoon.

At least the sun was out to keep me warm.

I didn't have to kick for long. A boat came alongside me. *Gaspar's Revenge.*

I hated to admit it, but I was glad to see him. Deuce was at the helm. He put her in neutral. Jesse leaned over the side. "Hey, you need a lift?" He started to reach down, then hesitated. "This is my last dry shirt," he said with a grin.

I rolled my eyes. "Really?"

The next wave lifted me, breaking over my head. Jesse grabbed hold of my arm, wrist to wrist, and lifted me right out of the water and onto the gunwale. I swung my legs over and sat down on the floor with my legs crossed, exhausted.

Finn greeted me with wet kisses and a wagging tail. He had on a doggie life vest.

"Where's Dalton?" Jesse asked.

"So much for small talk," I said. I nuzzled Finn with my nose. "Is he always like this?"

"He's your partner, right?"

"Yeah, but—I dunno," I said. Why was it his business anyway? I hollered up to Deuce, "Is he gone?"

Deuce nodded. "Hightailing it out of here."

Good. To Jesse, I said, "I was just working a lead. On my own."

"Uh-huh." Jesse eyed me, not believing a word I said. "You've gone rogue."

"Well, that depends on your definition of—"

"We watched you out there," he said, pointing aft. "Throwing whatever it was at their boat. What the hell are you up to?"

I looked at Finn and he stared back at me with his big, amber eyes. Damn.

"Stink bombs," I said. "We hit them with stink bombs, okay."

"Stink bombs," he repeated.

"Dalton and I don't agree on the course of action, exactly. So, I was doing my own thing."

"Uh-huh." Jesse stared at me. He wasn't going to let up. "And?"

"And, I admit, I'm a little unorthodox. But hey, I've got a pretty good track record." I pursed my lips. "Mostly."

"Uh-huh." This time he eased back, leaned against the gunwale, crossed his arms, and sized me up, as though trying to carefully plan his next words. Opening the mini-fridge, he took out two water bottles and handed me one. "And what exactly was the purpose of this unorthodox stink bomb attack? If you don't mind me asking, of course."

"It was cover," I said as I tipped the bottle and chugged down a couple swallows. "Thanks." I wiped my mouth with the back of my hand. "I needed to get close to the boat to disable their"—what had Rod called it?—"diver recall transducer."

"Why?" he said, staring at my lips.

"Because I learned that's how they communicate with the dolphins. They can summon them anytime they want, from great distances."

"Wish you'd've mentioned it. We have one on board. We could've blasted a signal to cancel theirs."

I stared up at him. Of course he could've done that. "But for how long?"

He gave me a half shrug.

"I had to destroy it."

"Uh-huh." He took a swig of his own water, eyed me. "I'm going to take a stab in the dark and guess that Dalton didn't think this was a good idea."

Men. I drew in a breath. Exhaled. "You know, a ride back to the dock would be greatly appreciated. Thank you."

"Sure thing, little lady."

He didn't say anything more. Finished his water and climbed the ladder to the bridge.

I stayed where I sat, with my arm around Finn. He seemed to enjoy my company and I needed a friend right now. I'd accomplished my goal—I got the sound amplifier—but I still needed to get the tracker off the fifth dolphin and I had no idea how I was going to do it.

"Maybe you could help," I said to the dog. "Lure her in with your puppy-dawg eyes, then bite it right off of her fin. Hey, you'd earn your name."

He licked my cheek.

"It's all right, boy. I'll take care of it," I said, giving Finn a squeeze. "I'll figure it out."

I had to.

Once the boat started bouncing through the waves, Finn found a more stable spot to curl up and snooze.

I sat back and closed my eyes, letting the sun warm me. One more tracker off, and they'd be free. From the Russians and the Americans.

Around the north side of the island, Jesse brought the boat to a slow idle and tucked close to some deep-water mangroves.

I got to my feet. There'd been no mention of a stop. "What's up? Where're we going?" I asked.

He brought the boat to a halt in a shallow, sandy spot.

"Finn's gotta take a whiz," he said.

I looked down at the dog, curled up in a ball, sound asleep.

Jesse hit a button on the dash and the anchor chain creaked to life—kak, kak, kak.

Finn sprang to all fours.

"See?" Jesse grinned.

Finn paced, his tail wagging.

Once Jesse had the anchor set, he killed the engine, climbed down from the cockpit, and opened the transom door.

He removed Finn's life vest. "Find us something to snack on while you're out there," he told him, rubbing his ears.

The dog gave him an affirmative bark and jumped into the

water, completely submerging for a second before popping up, his front legs dog-paddling to keep him afloat.

Looking around, he spotted the shoreline and struck out toward it at a fast swim, using his thick tail as a rudder.

Jesse said. "So, how long have you and Dalton been working together?"

"About a year and a half," I said, watching Finn.

"Yeah? How's it going?"

Did this guy ever let up? "Right now? Well…"

"Uh-huh."

Finn reached the beach and trotted out onto the sand, his nose to the ground.

"What was that about the snack?" I asked.

"You like clams?"

"No."

"That's right. Deuce mentioned you pitched the conch I bought you."

"He had eyes on me, huh?"

Jesse nodded.

"Yeah, well, sorry about that. I'm a vegetarian. I was so caught up in—doesn't matter."

Finn disappeared into the mangroves.

"Right now, I think he's just looking to relieve himself," Jesse said, as though it were a momentary delay and he'd soon be on snack patrol.

A moment later, Finn returned to the water's edge. He paced back and forth on the wet sand, stopping to sniff at it here and there, before he waded back into the water and began pawing around at the bottom with his big front paws. The water around him quickly silted over. I swear he drew in a big breath before shoving his head under water. When he came up, he had a clam in his mouth. He started swimming back toward the boat.

"I've never seen anything like that," I said.

"Yeah, he's something to behold." Jesse crossed his arms and turned to face me. "You were saying, about you and Dalton?"

Why was he so interested? "You know how it is. Sometimes you don't see eye to eye."

He held my gaze. "Looks more like a lover's quarrel to me."

Dammit. I shook my head. "Oh, we aren't—"

His hands shot up in front of him and he looked at me with soft, knowing eyes. "Not my circus, not my monkeys." He leaned forward for emphasis. "It's obvious the man cares about you. A lot. In case you didn't know."

Why was everyone feeling compelled to tell me this?

He just looked down at me, his eyes moving back and forth to each of mine, waiting.

I crossed my arms in front of my chest.

"And I can see you are one stubborn woman." He feigned a wince. "I've known a few like you over the years. Fierce. Lord almighty." His gaze turned inward for a brief moment, then he was back. "Anyway, I can't stand by and watch you get yourself killed. Those men out there are Russian military. This ain't a game."

Heat rose up my neck. "Thanks for the advice."

He frowned. "What I'm saying is—"

"Yeah, I got the picture."

He stared at me. Frowned again.

Finn reached the swim platform and deposited his clam, then turned and swam in circles for a moment, then dove under. Down to the bottom he went, and pawed at the sand a moment. He must have been six feet down to the bottom. When he came back up, he had another clam in his mouth.

"Good boy," Jesse shouted, as he dropped it on the platform with the other one.

He turned and dove again.

"Your dog's cute. But I'd really like that ride back to the dock now, please."

Jesse sighed. "Sure thing. C'mon, Finn."

Finn climbed up onto the swim platform, and Jesse headed back up to the helm. He looked down and waited till Finn clumsily moved his clams into the bucket.

"Mind closing the door?" Jesse asked.

I reached for it, started to give it a shove, then caught myself. Why was I so aggravated? I drew in a breath. Exhaled. I glanced at Jesse. He really was a nice guy.

I carefully closed the door and hitched the latch.

Dalton was standing on the dock when we pulled in. Deuce must have called him on the marine radio. *Great.*

He stood, hands on his hips, that look on his face, but when he spoke, his voice was calm. "What exactly were you doing out there?"

"My job," I said.

He set his eyes on me. "Without informing your partner. Without backup. Without any kind of—"

I held up my hand to stop him. "I already got the fifth degree from him." I jabbed my thumb over my shoulder toward Jesse.

His gaze shifted to something over my shoulder, then back to me. The muscles in his neck drew taut. "I have no idea what's going on with you. You're not making any sense. You're not listening to sense. You're going off on your own, half-cocked. It's like when we first met. I thought we'd worked past this."

"Yeah, well, like you said, we agreed to disagree. We're not always going to see eye-to-eye. And since I don't even know what's happening with this partnership thing, what's going on, anyway…"

He stepped back, stared at me.

I looked away.

"We need to talk," he said.

"Yes, I'm sure we do."

He straightened up. "While you've been *out*, we got a hold of Hyland."

Oh. "The phones are back on?"

He stared at me, deadpan.

"Right, of course. What did she say?"

He stepped closer, making sure only I could hear him. "She said to stand down."

"What!" I couldn't believe it. "Stand down?"

"Shhh." His eyes darted back and forth. "Believe me, I'm as disappointed as you are. But her exact words were, *do not engage.*"

I stared at him, stunned. This couldn't be. Finally, I said, "I don't believe you."

His eyebrows shot up. "What? Are you kidding? Why would I—" He exhaled with a heavy whoosh. "She said to leave the island on the next plane."

"But that doesn't make sense."

Through clenched teeth, he said, "Why does that matter?"

"Why does that *matter*? Because we have a job to do. I still have to get the fifth—"

"Our *job* is to do whatever she tells us to do. It doesn't have to make sense."

"But—"

"But nothing. Let's go." He took me by the arm.

I yanked free. "Wait." I spun to face him. "Look me in the eyes and tell me you don't agree with me. Tell me you don't."

"It doesn't matter what I agree with or don't. We're going."

"No. I'm not going anywhere."

"Poppy, c'mon. What's gotten into you? We've talked

about this."

"No. You've talked. I can't leave and do nothing."

The muscles in his jaw tightened. "But your job—"

"Well, then my job sucks." I crossed my arms. "I signed up to help animals. To bust bad guys. To right the wrongs. How is leaving now going to do that?"

"We don't always know the bigger picture."

"What a bunch of crap. *The bigger picture?* The bigger picture doesn't take into account the welfare of *these* five dolphins and you know it. You said it yourself."

"Poppy, we're talking about international warfare. This could be way bigger than we know."

"Yeah, and why is that? Why can't we be *in the know*? This isn't the military. I didn't join the military, where I'm supposed to blindly, unquestioningly, follow orders. Why the hell am I even here if my hands are going to be tied? Huh, why?"

He stared.

"Those dolphins have been taken captive, against their will, and trained to be soldiers. And—"

He shook his head.

"What?"

"I just…knew you wouldn't be able to…"

"What? I wouldn't be able to what?"

"Nothing."

I clamped my jaw shut.

He glared at me. "You don't get it, do you?"

"Gee, I bet you're going to explain it to me." I was pissed and I didn't care if I was being snarky.

He paused. I could tell he was restraining himself. "Those dolphins are worth thousands, tens of thousands of dollars to the Russian government. You think taking away their audio device is going to stop them? That they're just going to sail away and forget the whole project? They'll have a new device here within hours, that is, if they don't already have a backup on board."

I drew back. *Dammit, Jesse.*

"Yeah, I know what you've been up to. Getting the trackers off the dolphins' fins, which—good work by the way—but you think *that's* going to make a difference for these dolphins? There's still a tracker on one right? Your researcher said they travel in groups. They'll stay together. They only need the one to track the whole group. You've been running around making trouble, but you've accomplished nothing."

"That's not true." My knees felt weak.

"It is true and you know it."

I stared, trying not to give away what I was feeling. "What'd you tell Hyland?"

He crossed his arms. "Nothing."

"Tom and Mike know I got the trackers."

"They won't say anything. The Russians likely suspect what you wanted them to suspect, that you're a hot-headed activist. The hot-headed part sure as hell is right on target."

"And so everything will go on as it was. We get on a plane and leave. We stand down."

"Exactly."

"But what about Kerrie? She's still in danger."

He stared. I could tell he was pondering that one, but he wouldn't admit it. "As long as she stays quiet, she'll be fine."

They travel in groups. They'll stay together. They only need the one to track the whole group...

Dalton shook his head. "Oh no. Whatever you're thinking, the answer is no."

"What if there was a way to save the dolphins *and*—"

"Poppy, you can't just—"

"No, hear me out. I have an—"

"No. You hear me out. I can't do this anymore."

"What?" I stepped back. "What are you saying?"

It was there, in his eyes. "I'm done." He turned and walked away.

CHAPTER 20

"He'll cool down. He's Dalton. He just needs a minute," Chris said. He slid over and patted the couch cushion next to him.

I plopped down and leaned into him. "I don't know. He seemed…" How did he seem? I'd never seen him react that way. Something was very…wrong. "He's been exasperated with me before. Many times. Well, all the time, actually. But not like this."

Chris wrapped his arms around me. "I'm sure it's going to be fine."

"I'm supposed to be on the next plane."

"What do you mean?" He pulled away. "Why?"

"My boss said to stand down. Leave. It's over. She doesn't care about the dolphins."

His eyebrows slammed together. "What? I don't understand."

"It's political bullshit. What's to understand?"

He seemed to accept this. "So, what are you gonna do?"

"Maybe Jesse was right. I'm in over my head. I can't go after Russian-trained military operatives. Not alone."

"Who says you're alone?"

"Chris, I love you. I can't ask you to—"

He pulled back, shaking his head. "Not me. Hell no. This Jesse guy. And that Deuce. I bet they have the skills to make those Russian dudes disappear."

"Yeah, I'm sure you're right. But even if they would, that would make things worse." I snuggled into Chris's embrace. "What I really need is for the dolphins to disappear."

My body tingled all over. I jerked up straight. That was it.

"Chris!" I grabbed him by the back of his head, pulled him toward me, and kissed him on the lips. "You're a genius!"

"I am?"

"I know what to do."

"You do?"

"Yeah." I grinned.

He frowned. "Will I get shot at again?"

"I don't think so."

"All right then. Let's get to it. One of these days, I've got to get back to work."

I went right through the back door of Kerrie's house without knocking.

She leapt to her feet when she saw me.

"Is there someplace on the island you can go for a few days?"

"What?" She moved toward her kids who played on the living room floor. "What's going on?"

"Change in plans and"—her little girl looked up at me with big, round eyes—"and I just want to be sure you're safe. Just for a day or two."

"I guess, I—"

"Good. Get packed."

She gathered her kids close and went straight to the bedroom.

Natalie was sitting at the kitchen table, her eyes wide. "What's going on?"

"Glad you're here," I said. "You're just who I need to talk to. I have to catch the last dolphin." If the Russians hadn't already shot her. "We need that tracker. No matter what, we have to have it. What do we do?"

"Well,—" her eyes traveled around the surface of the table as she thought "—if we really have to, we could dart it. I guess?"

"We can? I thought you only observed the dolphins here. I didn't think you'd have anything like that."

"We do, but we have one on hand in case a dolphin gets entangled in abandoned fishing gear or something like that. There's often no other way to get them unentangled because they'll fight us. "

"Well, let's get to it."

She rose from the chair and we headed for the door.

On the way, Natalie explained the procedure. We'd need to get within forty feet of the dolphin before firing the dart. And that was if she wasn't moving, or one of us was a good shot. All while bobbing in the ocean.

"I'll do it," I said. I'd won the firearm medal in agent training. I was confident I could hit the mark. Though this was a CO2 gun, similar to a paintball gun, but I'd also shot those in training.

The dart would penetrate the dolphin's thick layer of blubber and inject the drug directly into the muscle. Once the sedative took effect—a light sedative, Natalie assured me—the dolphin would become lethargic, but not fall asleep completely. If she did, she would drown. We'd have to catch her quickly and keep her afloat until she regained full consciousness.

"How will we do that?" I asked.

"I don't know. We've only darted one, that I was around for, but it was entangled. So, we didn't have to catch it."

"We'll have to wing it."

She nodded.

Chris agreed to take the wheel again, freeing me and Natalie to work with the dolphin.

If we found her. Alive.

It was late afternoon now and the sun would be up for only a few more hours.

We sped out toward the spot where we'd seen them during the storm, where I'd removed the other four trackers, but there was no sign of them.

Natalie suggested another area where they'd been spotted hanging out the week before.

Chris turned the wheel and headed that way.

They weren't in that area either.

We searched every spot Natalie knew, but we didn't see the dolphins.

The fact was, they were most likely hanging close to the Russian boat. Where I couldn't get to them.

"Meet me here at dawn?" I said, back at the dock.

Natalie and Chris were discouraged, but agreed.

"What are you going to do now?" Chris asked.

"It's time to call in the cavalry," I said and left them. I headed straight to the marina, to *Droppin' Skirts*. I needed some ammo first. If I was lucky, Dalton wouldn't be there.

Tom was aboard, alone, cleaning dishes from his dinner. Red Hot Chili Peppers played on the radio.

"Where's Mike?" I asked.

"Ah, he was anxious to get back to the states. Took the next plane when Hyland gave the nod. I told him I'd take the boat back. Why not?"

"Sure. A little fun in the sun."

"That why you're still here?" He wiped his hands with a dish towel and opened the tiny refrigerator. "Want a beer?"

"Yeah. Sun. No beer. Thanks. I, uh, promised Kerrie I'd

give her some info on the dolphins though, before I left. For her research. Any chance you recorded that call? The one you detected when the dolphins turned away from me?"

He headed toward the hydrophone equipment. "Well, I assume so. That was the protocol." He pulled a memory stick from the hydrophone device and plugged it into a laptop. "Let's see."

In a few minutes, he had all the tracks pulled up. "Here it is. There's a date and time stamp."

"Great, thanks. I know she'll appreciate it," I said, pocketing the stick.

"Listen," he said, eyeing me, treading carefully. "I know you weren't happy with the way this all came down."

"Oh, no. No, no worries. We can't win 'em all, right?" I gave him a grin.

"Right," he said, crossing his arms. "It's just...I agreed with you. I wanted you to know that. I didn't think it was right."

"Well, I appreciate that, Tom."

He exhaled, as though he'd been holding his breath, waiting for my reaction. "I'm going to head back to Miami first thing in the morning. I guess we'll all take a breather and regroup when Hyland gives us the call, eh?"

"Yeah. Yeah," I said. But my stomach clenched tight. I wasn't sure how I could work for Hyland after this. Another thing I had to think over when all this was done.

"Dalton must be in Montana by now."

"He—what?"

"Well—" He paused, eyeing me. "He left before Mike did. You didn't know he was gone?"

"Oh, yeah," I lied, nodding too much. *Dalton left? Without a word? No goodbye?* "I just didn't realize he was able to catch the earlier flight. Good for him."

Suddenly I couldn't draw in air.

"Anyway, catch you later." I spun, turning my backside to

him so he couldn't read my face.

Why would he do that? It's not like we'd had a fight. Not a real fight. But he'd just...*left?*

Deep breath. I couldn't think about that right now. I needed to do this one thing, for the dolphins. Then I could think about that. About Dalton. As soon as I was done here.

CHAPTER 21

Gaspar's Revenge was still tied to the dock. Lights glowed inside.

I jumped aboard, walked straight into the salon. Jesse and a blond woman were seated at the settee. They both looked up quickly from a laptop, their hands moving in unison; his to a sidearm I was sure was tucked under his shirt. He relaxed when he recognized me and held a hand up to the woman.

"What the hell?"

My eyes went from his to hers. Obviously, I'd just barged in on something. She was very pretty, dark tanned, several years older than me, but very fit, almost a female version of Jesse.

My eyes fixed on his. "I need your help."

He cocked his head to the side. "Well, okay."

The woman had an amused expression on her face as Jesse rose, told her he'd return in a moment, and walked me back out to the dock.

"Boarding without permission could get you shot," he offered.

"Sorry, but I really need your help."

He stopped and turned toward me, eyes waiting.

"Tonight, would you and Deuce do your recon-incursion-thing you do with those fancy rebreathers you have, and foul the prop on that Russian boat?"

With skepticism in his eyes, he slowly nodded. "He's gone.

But I might."

"You can do that alone?"

Now he looked at me amused, one eyebrow arching. "Uh, yeah."

"Okay." This wasn't going as I'd planned. "Didn't mean to offend."

"No offense taken."

"All right then. Um. Don't use a dock line. Has to be something they'd get entangled in by accident. Plastic, old fishing net, something."

"Uh-huh."

I handed him the memory stick. "Then, at dawn, would you play the sounds that my team recorded through your diver recall system? It's track seven."

Again, he nodded slowly. "I could."

"If we can call in the last dolphin, we can get her satellite transmitter off."

The eyebrow nudged upward again. "Her?"

"Yeah, well, she's the clever one, I figure she must be female."

He grinned. "Right."

"I'll meet you out there," I said. "You play the pied piper and I'll do the rest."

He stared, looking into my eyes, considering something.

"Will you do it?"

"For you?"

"For the dolphins?"

He gave me a big smile.

I couldn't resist planting a kiss on his cheek.

Dalton didn't answer when I called. Not one of the seven times. Maybe his phone had died.

Maybe there would be a million dollars in my bank account

when I woke up.

Maybe I'd already lost my mind and didn't have the capacity to realize it. Is that what happened when people lost their marbles? They had no idea until they found themselves locked in a white room, bound in a straight jacket, thinking, hm, how'd I get here? Oh yeah. I must have lost my marbles.

I held my head in my hands. *Get yourself together!*

It was better this way. Dalton wouldn't be happy with me. Not in the long run. He'd expect me to settle down, be someone else. And I couldn't do that. It just wouldn't work. That's all. It wouldn't work. I wasn't a white-picket fence kind of gal. Two point three kids and a dog. Well, I could definitely have a dog. But that wasn't the point. Married? A family? A yard to mow? No, it was better this way.

I found the Benadryl in the bottom of my bag, took three, shut the lights out, and stared at the water-stained ceiling tile, lit by the faint orange glow of the streetlight, for the next six hours.

At dawn, Chris, Natalie, and I set out again in the Zodiac. The waves were less than three feet and there wasn't a cloud in the sky. As the sun rose, it seemed to warm everything.

Rounding the island, I caught site of *Gaspar's Revenge* on the horizon, heading our way.

The closer we got to him, the more we slowed, concerned the dolphins might be nearby.

Jesse waved from the flying bridge and gave me a thumbs up. I could see astern, five dorsal fins breaking the surface. He had them! And number five was with them!

I let out a gleeful woop.

"Let's get the dart gun ready," I said to Natalie.

"Tell him to slow down. They're moving too fast to dart."

I raised my hand and gave Jesse a thumbs down, the universal sign to reduce his speed.

He got the message and throttled back.

Chris drove the Zodiac in a big circle, giving the dolphins lots of space, and fell in behind *Gaspar's Revenge.*

Natalie handed me the gun, already cocked and loaded. "Don't miss," she said. "We only have one."

"Okay, no pressure," I said with a nervous grin.

Chris followed Jesse, matching his speed. I got the tagged dolphin in my sights.

"Hold her steady," I said to Chris.

"Roger that. Holdin' her steady."

The five dolphins swam in a synchronized motion. Three fins appeared, then the other two. Then they were under for four seconds. Then three fins appeared, then the other two. My target swam on the right flank in the first three.

I watched, counted. One-two-three-four. Three fins, then two. One-two-three-four. Three fins, then two. I held the weapon steady against my shoulder, using my knees as shock absorbers to compensate for the boat's movement, and aimed where the dolphins should appear next. One-two-three-four. Three fins. On an exhale, I squeezed the trigger. The dart flew. I looked up. The dolphin was gone.

"Did I hit her?"

Natalie shook her head. "I don't know. I think you missed."

Dammit!

"We only had one dart."

The three fins broke the surface. One dolphin had a red dart stuck right below the dorsal fin. Right where I'd aimed.

"Yes!"

Natalie cheered.

"Great shot, Poppy!" Chris said.

Jesse pumped his fist in the air, cheering me on.

Chris kept pace with the dolphin, staying alongside her as she slowed.

"She's getting sleepy," Natalie warned. "Stay close. We can't let her sink."

The other dolphins slowed as she slowed, staying with her.

"How do we get close enough to get the sling under her?" I asked.

Natalie watched the dolphin with intense concern.

"What are you thinking?" I pressed.

"We've got to time this perfectly."

"Okay, talk to me," I said. "What do you mean?"

"Well, we need to get right in there the moment she's so sleepy she's starting to sink, but not too early, because she might dive, or struggle against us. She probably weighs over six hundred pounds, so…"

"Okay," I said. "How will we know?"

She shook her head, concern in her eyes. "I don't know. I didn't…I mean, I've never done this."

Oh crap. "Well, all right. Are you saying that—what are you saying?"

She shook her head some more and started wringing her hands.

"If we could get the sling under her…?"

The sling was a basic canvas stretcher, customized for a dolphin.

"But to lift it…" She stared, not finishing her sentence.

The dolphin slowed. Made a lazy exhalation.

I grabbed fins, a mask and snorkel. "I'll get in the water," I said.

Natalie shook her head. "If she bucks, and throws her peduncle, she could kill you."

"Tie a line to this side of the sling," I told her.

She did as I asked.

I signaled to Jesse to put his boat in neutral.

"Chris, use the Zodiac to keep her corralled against the other boat. All right?"

"Roger that," he said as I jumped into the water.

When I popped back up to the surface, I hollered to Natalie, "Lower the sling."

I took hold of one end and dove with it, pulling it downward, under the dolphin.

The other dolphins zipped back and forth in a frenzy.

I needed to get the sling under one dolphin. I could do that. Maybe. If she'd stop moving. And the others would get out of the way.

Then beside me, a figure appeared. It was Jesse. He gave me a thumbs up and took hold of the other side of the sling.

The dolphin was above us, slowly pushing through the water like she'd had too much tequila.

Jesse gestured to me, miming how we'd come up, simultaneously, on either side of the dolphin. I nodded that I understood.

He gave the sling a tug, and up we went. As I emerged next to the dolphin, the canvas snugged beneath her belly. Jesse was on her other side. She wiggled side to side, but it was a lazy effort. We quickly tied the straps atop her back that held the sling in place.

Chris was right there with the Zodiac. I tossed the dangling line to Natalie and moved out of the way as Jesse helped push the dolphin alongside the boat. Natalie secured both ends of the sling to the plastic cleats on the Zodiac.

"That will keep her snug while the sedative wears off," she said, relief in her voice. "Good job guys!"

Gaspar's Revenge was much easier to climb aboard from the water, so I followed Jesse that way.

Finn met me with a wagging tail and wet kisses. I gave him a quick scratch behind his ears.

"Thanks for all your help," I said to Jesse, dripping on the transom.

He shrugged it off. "It was either that or watch you drown."

"What? I could've—"

"I'm kidding." He gave me a grin and I was reminded how handsome he was. "You're obviously a more-than-capable young lady."

"I don't know how you'd know that. I swear, I've been benched this whole operation. Not to mention my head has been—" He was looking at me with a grin. "Forget it."

"I don't know anything about that," he said. "But I do know, a good agent knows how to best use the tools at her disposal. In this case, well, it's been me." He paused. "Did I just call myself a tool?"

I nodded. "Thanks. I figured you'd say something wise like, know thyself," I said with a wink.

That made him laugh. "Yeah, that's what I meant."

We stared at each other for an uncomfortable moment. I knew he was attracted to me. And I was to him. But…

"Hey, about Africa. I was wondering if you knew anything about what was going on in the South Sudan round about the time—"

"What's all this about Africa? Why do you and Dalton have so much interest?"

"What do you mean? Dalton asked about it?"

His expression changed. No doubt, he regretted letting that slip. He knew I wasn't going to let it pass. "Dalton asked me about it is all. My time there."

"Africa?"

"Just general stuff." He tried to blow it off.

"I got it!" Natalie hollered, getting our attention. She held the satellite transmitter up to show she'd removed it from the dolphin's fin.

I gave her a thumbs up.

To Jesse, I said, "As soon as that dolphin is swimming on her own again, I've got to go."

"I had a feeling there might be a few more steps in your plan."

"You'll keep them away from the Russian boat for the rest of the day?"

"An easy promise," he said. "I can't think of anything I'd rather do."

I gave him a kiss on the cheek. "I knew you weren't an evil drug runner."

He grinned. "And I knew you weren't an ornithology intern."

"What?" I grinned. "I know a lot about birds. I could pull that off."

"No doubt in my mind," he said.

Africa... "So when Dalton was asking—"

"She's already waking up," Natalie shouted.

I glanced at her. *Damn.* "I gotta go," I told Jesse.

He nodded.

I threw my arms around him. "Thanks. I mean it."

"You take care of yourself," he whispered in my ear. "And take it from me: true love doesn't come along very often. So, don't blow it."

I pulled away, looked into his eyes, and saw the genuine concern he felt for me.

"Right," I said, my cheeks blushing pink.

"I mean it." He held my gaze. "When you get to be my age, you know these things. Right now, you think your career is everything. You gotta make something of yourself, got something to prove. But in the end, it's the people we love, our relationships that matter." He stared at me as though, if he could make me see his point of view by sheer will, he would.

I nodded. If I admitted it to myself, I could easily see my life without being an agent. But I couldn't envision a world without Dalton.

"We need your help," Chris shouted from the other boat.

I swung around. They were trying to get the sling untied as the dolphin pushed from side to side, slamming against the boat, trying to escape. I turned back to Jesse. "Are you some kind of guardian angel? I ask, because, last night, I was sure I'd lost my marbles."

He laughed, a low hearty chuckle. "Actually, I've been called that before." He headed for the helm. "Let's get you back on that Zodiac."

The engines on *Gaspar's Revenge* rumbled to life and Jesse brought the stern around so I could step off onto the Zodiac.

In a few moments, we had the dolphin's sling untied and she dove deep, then sprang from the depths into the air, only to fall back with a splash. The other four dolphins frolicked about her, chattering away.

"They're free," Natalie said. "They know it. I know they know it." She blushed when she turned to me, worry in her eyes. "Don't tell anyone I said that. I'll lose my cred as a scientist."

"Mum's the word," I told her, grinning.

CHAPTER 22

I asked Chris to head around the north side of the island, keeping our speed below ten miles per hour, while Natalie got Kerrie on the phone. She passed it to me and I told her where to meet us and the details of my plan.

An hour and twenty minutes later, Chris landed the Zodiac on shore, right where the dolphin had been stranded a few days ago.

Kerrie was already there. "You're sure this will work?"

"It's our best shot. I destroyed the other four transmitters after I got them," I told her. "Had I known... But this should work. Like you said, this one was the leader. The others would follow. They'd know that."

She nodded.

"And you trust your team? They'll keep a good patrol. No one will see inside?"

"It'll work," she said, her face tight with worry. "It's gonna work."

Three golf carts pulled up with a crew of local men. Within minutes they had several tents set up.

"Make sure the side walls are attached so no one can see inside," I said, handing her the transmitter.

Kerrie entered the tent with it, shouting orders to get the side walls hung.

"What can we do?" Natalie asked.

"Keep your fingers crossed that this works."

I got on the marine radio and hailed *Gaspar's Revenge*.

Jesse answered and had me switch from the universal emergency and hailing channel to channel seventeen.

I repeated the channel, "One seven, switching to channel one seven," enunciating clearly for anyone else who might be listening on the airwaves.

On seventeen, I called for him again.

"*Gaspar's Revenge* here," he came back.

"Jesse. Can you come help? Some dolphins have beached themselves."

"What? That's terrible. What can we do?"

"We need men to help carry buckets, to keep them cool. I don't know though, they're in bad shape, really distressed."

"Tell me where."

"The beach on the north side of the island. Inside the bay."

"Okay. Keep your chin up. I'll be there as soon as I can."

I pictured Jesse, idling along through the waves, grinning while five dolphins followed his boat.

I gave Kerrie a thumbs up. "That ought to get those Russians running over here for confirmation."

Assuming they got their prop untangled by now. I grinned, satisfied with myself.

I fired up the hotspot on my phone. "Okay, part two."

She flipped open her laptop. "I'll post on the forum first."

With a few clicks, she posted an announcement on the Marine Biology Network forum:

Five Bottlenose Dolphins Stranded in Bimini.

Five *Tursiops* have stranded and perished. Cause unknown.
Initial hypothesis: stress-related.
Autopsies ordered. Results will be posted.

Next, we drafted a press release. Simple and to the point. No need to add any details. News of five dead dolphins would hit the AP and be picked up all over the U.S. and beyond.

"I hate to lie. I mean, I'm a scientist," Kerrie said, her face drawn.

"I know. Me too. But it's for all the right reasons."

"I know," she said and hit the send button. As she looked up, her eyes narrowed. "Oh no," she whispered.

The Russian vessel had rounded the buoy and was heading into the bay. I guess they got the prop unbound and working again.

"It's all right. This is part of the plan," I assured her. "I'll take care of it. Make sure the patrol volunteers are in place, then stay in the tent."

With a nod, she picked up her laptop and ducked inside.

"You too," I said to Chris and Natalie.

I sat in a lawn chair, my legs crossed, sipping from my water bottle as I watched them set anchor. Then one got into their dinghy and headed my way. My old friend, the stalker.

I got up from the chair and timed my arrival at the water's edge to match his.

"This is your fault!" I shouted, jabbing my finger at him. "You harassed these dolphins. I saw you. They're dead and it's all your fault. I know what you were doing."

The man scowled as he quickly scanned for anyone who might have noticed my outburst.

"I'm going to tell everyone, if it's the last thing I do."

His neck turned red, giving him away.

I crossed my arms in front of my chest and stared, daring him to speak.

Looking past me, trying to get a glimpse of the dead dolphins, he said in a calm, restrained tone, "You are wrong. We did nothing."

"Well, I don't believe you," I said, making my voice shake. "And they're dead now."

"I want to see," he said, moving toward the tents.

"I already tried," I said to his backside, restraining myself from tackling him. "No one's allowed in."

He waved a hand, blowing me off. "I am scientist."

"Yeah, well, me too. And they said absolutely not. It's like a hazardous zone or something."

As he approached the tent, a man blocked his way—a six foot two, three hundred pound tower of pure muscle—his arms crossed in front of his chest. After I'd told Kerrie what to expect might happen, she'd called him. Davy was his name. He loaded the ferry during the day and bounced unruly tourists from one of the local bars at night.

The Russian slowed.

Davy shook his head.

With a huff, he spun on me.

"Told you," I said, all snotty.

"Let me in. I demand it." He couldn't contain his fury. His lips were pursed tight, his ears turning red.

"Enough. Now you calm down," I said, my voice dripping with sweet sarcasm while I threw his words back in his face.

That really set him off. He turned back toward Davy, as if to charge, but then backed off when Davy gave him the slightest shake of his head.

The man spun back around to me. As his mouth opened to speak, I grinned and said, "Go ahead, call me a stupid girl one more time."

He looked like he was brewing enough steam that his head might launch from his neck.

I grinned and his eyes flashed with frustration. He knew I had him.

The flap on the tent opened and Kerrie stepped out. What was she doing? She tugged rubber gloves from her hands before she wiped her brow with the back of her hand. As if she'd just noticed him, she made eye contact with the Russian, then shook her head.

Good thinking, Kerrie!

His eyes darted from her to me and back before he turned and stomped back to his dingy. One shove, and he had it afloat and spun around facing out. He crawled aboard, pulled the starter on the little outboard engine, and headed back to his boat.

Davy gave me a nod. Kerrie looked like she might melt into a puddle right there on the sand.

I let out my breath.

Chris poked his head out from inside the tent. "Is he gone?"

"Yeah," I said. "Let's talk on the backside of the tent."

Kerrie and I left Davy on the lookout and moved out of sight to talk to Natalie and Chris.

"That was amazing," Natalie said. "You were amazing."

"I wanted to bash his skull in," I said, adrenaline still coursing through my veins.

"Well, I'm proud of you," Chris said.

"For what?"

"For not bashing his skull in."

"Let's hope this is the end of it," I told Kerrie. "Once they see the news on the wire, they'll believe it, even without the bodies."

"I hope so."

"I have a feeling they'll be hightailing it back to Cuba tonight."

"I don't know how to thank you."

"Easy. You'll keep me informed. How they're doing."

"I will," she said.

"The dolphins *and* your kids."

She smiled. "Will do."

CHAPTER 23

Chris and I headed back to the Hilton together, where he planned to check out and head back to his job.

"So, now what?" he said as soon as we were out of earshot.

"Now, I...I don't know."

"You said Hyland told you to get on the next plane."

"Yeah, well. I'm starting to wonder if..."

Chris gave me the look. "Wonder if what?"

"If this is what I'm really meant to do."

"Are you kidding? It's all you've ever wanted. It's all you ever talk about. Being an agent and fighting for animals."

"Well, that's just it. Am I? She told us to stand down. To stand down, Chris."

"Maybe there was another plan, something you don't know, something—"

"Dalton was right. It's not about the animals."

Chris walked beside me in silence for awhile. As we approached the Hilton, he said, "So, what are you going to do?"

"I don't know." I looked down at my hands. I couldn't look at him. I had no answer.

"Come up to my room with me. I've got something for you."

I looked up at him. "You do?"

"Yeah, c'mon."

In his room, he gathered the few things that weren't already in his suitcase, then sat down on the bed and plunked at the keyboard on his laptop.

"What are you doing?" I asked.

He held up a hand. "Hang on."

"But what—"

The hand. "Give me a sec."

I waited. Finally he made a big show of hitting return with his index finger. "I just sent you an email."

"You what? Why? I'm right here." What was up with him?

"Listen to me." He set the laptop on the bed beside him and rose to face me. "You've got this whole vision in your head about Dalton and marriage and, what did you say, being settled down. Did you ever ask him if that's what *he* wants?"

I stared. "Well…"

"Well, nothing. You didn't. You've been making all these assumptions."

"But Alison—"

"He's not married to Alison, and there's a reason."

"Well, yeah, she cheated on him and—"

"You don't know that's the reason they got divorced. Didn't he say something about realizing…something?"

I thought about it. He had.

"Maybe he doesn't want that either. Maybe he doesn't even want to be married. Maybe lots of things. But that crazy brain of yours has made this all complicated. More complicated than it needs to be."

I frowned. Was he right? He was usually right.

"Check your email. It's a plane ticket to Bozeman. Once there, I've got a reservation for a rental car set up in your name."

"Bozeman? Montana?"

"Isn't that where Dalton is from? Isn't that where he would have gone?"

"Well, yeah, probably, but I can't—"

"But nothing." His eyes softened. "Poppy, I love you, but sometimes—" He sighed. "I've been so worried about you I've knitted three sets of knockers." He took me in his arms and kissed me on the cheek. When he pulled away, he looked me in the eyes. "So, get your skinny ass on that plane."

After I packed my bag, I swung by the Bimini Big Game Club. I had one more thank you to deliver.

I found Rod and Alison lounging in chairs by the pool.

Alison sat up when she saw me approach.

I held up a hand to keep her from having to get up. "I just came by to say thank you."

"Did everything work out?" she asked.

"Yeah, thanks to you and Rod. I appreciate your help."

"Anytime," he said.

Alison's gaze went past me. "Where's Dalton?"

I glanced over my shoulder. Habit. "Oh, he had to head back home already. He, uh, yeah." I didn't know what else to say.

A look of concern crossed her face. She turned to Rod. "Would you give us a minute, honey?"

He looked confused for a moment, then seemed to realize that it didn't matter whether or not he knew what was going on, and did as he was asked. "I think I need another beer. Can I get you one?" he asked me.

"No, thanks," I said to his backside.

"Where's Dalton?" she asked before Rod was ten feet away.

"I don't know. We had a disagreement, I guess you'd call it, and he left. The job was done, so…"

"Where'd he go?"

"I don't know."

With a huff, she said, "He's in Montana."

"How do you know that?"

"Because I know Dalton. Here." She pulled a notepad from her purse and jotted down something, then handed me the paper. "That's his home address. Start there, but he'll be in the woods."

"Why are you…?"

"I told you. I want him to be happy."

I glanced in the direction that Rod had gone. "And you didn't want Rod to hear you say that?"

She followed my gaze. "No. I asked him to go because I wanted to ask your advice."

"My advice?" Was she serious?

"I don't know what to do."

I shifted from one foot to the other. "Okay."

"Rod didn't bring me here to swim with the dolphins." Her lip curled up as she held back tears. "That was a convenient excuse."

She hesitated, so I quietly said, "Why did he bring you here then?"

"He left me alone in the room and went to some meet up. About a job. He went with that Jesse and Deuce out in the middle of the ocean. It was all a big secret. That's the whole reason we came here."

"But I thought the post office—"

"Yeah, you and me both. It seems he couldn't stand the idea of settling down." She hugged her belly and the child that was growing there. "I should have known. Once a SEAL, always a SEAL. I don't know what I was thinking. I mean, I couldn't tame Dalton either."

"I'm not sure—"

She looked on the verge of tears. "What do I do?"

"I don't—I don't know."

The tears started down her cheeks.

I sat down on the chair next to her. "Maybe it isn't what you think."

"Oh, he explained it. He lied to me. Before we got married." She sat up straighter to look me in the eyes. "He's worth a fortune. Who knew? Not me."

"What? I don't understand."

"Rod. He's super rich. Inherited a ton of money. He even set up a foundation, some charity. And he bought this, like, luxury fishing boat." The tears started again. She dug around in her purse, pulled out a tissue, and blotted her eyes with it. "All without telling me a word. Who does that?"

"Well, maybe..." I had nothing. No kidding. *Who does that?* I felt for her. She didn't deserve this.

"He said he wanted to be sure I loved him for him, not the money."

"Well, I guess I can understand that." I cringed, hoping I hadn't overstepped. "Can't you?"

She shrugged. "I guess."

"You do love him, right?"

She nodded, crying.

"Well, Rod loves you. It's plain and simple. Anyone can see it," I said.

"Do you really think so?"

I nodded.

"Yeah, but, will it be enough?"

I took her hand in mine and squeezed. "I'm sure everything will work out," I said and hoped, with all my heart, that it would. "Maybe it won't look like you imagined. What relationship does? But when two people love each other, they make it work, right? My mom and dad did. My mom's a Navy admiral and my dad was a free-spirited wildlife photographer. Sometimes they fought like cats. But they were madly in love. They made it work."

"I don't know." She sniffled.

"I do," I said. "It's a job. Sure, Rod might find it meaningful, but at the end of the day, he knows it's our relationships that matter. The ones we love."

"Yeah?" She cocked her head to the side. "Sounds like you should take your own advice."

I sat back. "And I was really starting to like you." I grinned.

She smiled, but the tears kept flowing.

CHAPTER 24

Dalton's house was at the end of a long dirt road that wound through wooded hills along a river of raging white-water. When I found the mailbox and confirmed the street number, I turned into the drive. Ahead, a two-story timber-frame house gripped the edge of a bluff, overlooking the river valley.

It was exactly the kind of house I pictured Dalton living in.

I rolled to a stop, killed the engine, and got out of the car.

The air smelled of pine. A magpie called from the tree overhead—wock, wock wock-a-wock.

A light was on inside. I drew in a breath. It's just Dalton. Why are you so nervous?

I got to the door and clanked the brass knocker.

Footsteps approached across a wood floor.

The door swung open and a woman stood before me, staring with an annoyed look on her drawn face, a cigarette hanging at the edge of her mouth. A ratty T-shirt hung from her bony shoulders. She had on cotton sweatpants and thread-bare pink slippers. Her hair hadn't been washed in days.

"What the hell you doin' way out here?" she said. "I gave at the office."

She spun and the door slammed shut in my face.

I stood there for a moment, unsure what to do. Was that Dalton's mother? She seemed the right age. I dug the paper out of my pocket and double-checked the address. I was in the right place. At least, the address Alison had given me.

What the heck? I reached for the knocker and gave it another whack, whack, whack.

The door flung open again. This time, the woman held a shotgun, aimed at me.

Shit! My hands shot up in the air. "I, uh, I'm just looking for Dalton. Garrett Dalton."

Her gaze traveled down to my shoes and back up again. "Go away," she said and slammed the door again.

I backed away, off the porch.

What the hell? Is this why Dalton never mentioned his mom?

The distinctive hum of a car's engine came through the trees.

An old pick up, circa 1980, pulled up behind my rental car.

A woman got out, about the same age as the woman inside the house, only this woman had a round belly and graying hair pulled up into a bun. She reached for something in the bed behind the cab.

"Hello," I called, cautiously approaching.

She looked my way as she hauled a bag of groceries up and over the side of the truck. "Hello there." A kind smile brightened her face.

"I'm looking for Dalton."

"Oh, yeah?" She seemed surprised by that. "Well, you just missed him."

"I did?"

"He's hard to catch."

Don't I know it. "And you are…?"

She thrust her hand at me. "Sarah. I keep an eye on the place. And his mom."

"Ah, yeah. We just met. Briefly." So she was his mom. "I'm afraid that I scared her."

The woman looked at me. "What do you mean?"

"She had a firearm."

"Oh, that," she said with a half grin. "There aren't any shells in it."

Well, I didn't know that.

"What do you need with Dalton?"

"Oh, I work with him. I, just, needed to talk with him is all. I haven't been able to reach him, so..."

She came to a halt in front of me, seemed to assess my story. Then she nodded, as though affirming what she thought. "Makes sense. He forgot his phone."

"He did?"

"Sorry, I can't help you, though. He didn't say where he was headed, or when he'd be back. If you know Dalton, you know what I mean. He keeps everything close to the vest."

I nodded, trying not to show my disappointment. And he'd left his phone. He wouldn't forget that. He left it on purpose.

"Do you want to leave him a note?"

"Nah," I said, shaking my head. "I'll catch up with him. I'm sure he'll call in, once he realizes he left the phone."

I gazed out over the river into the forest behind. *Where'd you go, Dalton?*

My phone rang and I lurched forward.

Dalton? I read the display. It was Kerrie. "Excuse me," I said to the woman and stepped away as I answered. "Agent McVie."

"Poppy. I just wanted you to know, we spotted the dolphins today. They were crater feeding with some of our resident bottlenose—all five of them."

"Oh, that's great news."

"I think they're going to be fine. Thanks to you."

I smiled. My phone beeped. Another call. Hyland. "Excuse me, Kerrie, it's my boss beeping in." I switched to the other line. "Agent McVie."

"Good afternoon," she said. "I'm glad I caught you."

"Caught me?"

"Yes. You're in Montana, aren't you? With Dalton?"

How'd she—*dammit.* Greg's voice echoed in my head. *I've got your GPS coordinates, too.*

"No," I said. "Dalton's not here. I don't know where he is."

"Oh," she said, then a beat later, "well, he asked for some time off. I just figured…"

Time off? "He didn't mention that to me," I said. "How much time off?"

"A couple of weeks."

Two weeks? And he left his phone...

"Had I known I'd need you two to check on something out there, I wouldn't have approved it."

"Out here? What do you mean?"

"We got a report of a rash of wolf kills outside Yellowstone."

My teeth clenched. The way wolves get demonized angers me.

"The numbers are higher than the statistical average. The thing is, it's a political hornet's nest. I was hoping you two could do a little investigating under the radar. See what's really happening over there."

I still had a job. But did I want it? Would this be just like the dolphins? Go in, get information, then leave the wolves to fend for themselves? Maybe I needed a vacation too. "You know, I think—"

"I want you to run point on this one."

"Really?"

"Get in there, assess the situation. However we move forward will be your call."

"I'll be in charge of this op?"

"Yeah, unless you feel you need Dalton to—"

"I don't need Dalton."

I don't need Dalton. The words felt sour as they came out of my mouth.

Author's Note

Well, that fulfilled one of my BIG dreams—to write a Poppy novel about dolphins. Thanks for coming along for the adventure.

Believe it or not, most everything in this story is TRUE in real life WITH THE EXCEPTION of Russian dolphins escaping from Cuba to Bimini. But the part about Russians (and the U.S.) using dolphins for military purposes is absolutely true. The articles mentioned in the book are real and online if you want to look them up.

The history of drug running from Bimini is true. The Dolphin House is a real place (super cool). Even the part I mentioned about a sheik who has a cheetah for a pet is true.

When I had the idea that the dolphins would willingly present their dorsal fins to Poppy to have their transmitters removed, I imagined, with no scientific confirmation, that they would be intelligent enough to recognize what she was doing. Then, I saw a video about the shark expert, Cristina Zenato, who removes fishing hooks from the mouths of sharks. She claims they come to her now, when they need a hook removed. Amazing.

For this story, I made my own trip to Bimini to swim with dolphins. It was amazing. While I was there, I decided to adopt a dolphin. Her name: Poppy McVie. You can learn about her on the Dolphin Communication Project web site.

The first $750 profit from the sale of this book has supported her adoption. AND, the best part, I got to see her when I was there and I got some great video of her bow riding. Go to my online network at Fortheanimals.kimberlibindschatel.com/posts/a-dolphin-named-poppy-mcvie to check it out.

Thank YOU for reading. If you're interested in connecting with me online, I like to share travel stories (like my own trip to swim with dolphins in Bimini) and videos (Have you ever seen a napping sloth? This is exciting stuff!), my wildlife photos, and MORE! Please sign up for my newsletter at www.KimberliBindschatel.com. You'll be the FIRST to know about my new releases, too. (I have a special sign-up gift for you.) Join the adventure.

THANK YOU

During the writing of this story, I had help from some wonderful people. Kelly and Nicole of the Dolphin Communication Project not only welcomed me, answering all my questions with patience, but inspired me through their love and dedication to these dolphins.

Special thanks to Skylar and JP for the brainstorming dinner. It was such fun. I enjoyed every minute. Your enthusiasm was contagious. I thought you'd think I was nuts when I told you the plot included Russians.

Thanks to my good friend, Steve, for the chemical stuff. I know I threw you for a loop when I called and asked how to make a homemade stink bomb. I appreciate so much that you took me seriously.

To Rachel, thanks, as always, for keeping Poppy real and Katy Bertodatto, you've been a blessing, breathing new life into this series.

I am so thankful for my early readers—Mom and Alexa. And my proof readers—Cathy, Annie, and Lisa—you went above and beyond.

Special thank you to Wayne Stinnett for believing in me and my stories enough to become part of them. Our cross over has been so much fun. You inspired me right out of a big slump. I owe you big time.

I get to do this because of the loving support of my

husband. As always, thanks to my parents for raising me with a deep love of animals.

Most of all, thank YOU for reading and supporting this indie author.

ABOUT THE AUTHOR

Kimberli A. Bindschatel is a thrill seeker, travel adventurer, passionate animal lover, wildlife photographer and award-winning author of the Amazon Best-selling Poppy McVie Mystery series.

When she's not busting bad guys with her pen, she's out in the wilderness getting an adrenaline fix. She has rappelled down a waterfall in Costa Rica, rafted the Grand Canyon, faced down an Alaskan grizzly bear at ten feet (camera in hand), snorkeled with stingrays, and white-water kayaked a Norwegian river. She's always ready for an adventure.

She lives in northern Michigan where she loves to hike in the woods with her rescue dog, Josee, share a bottle of wine with good friends, or sail Lake Michigan with her husband on their boat, Priorities. (You gotta have your priorities!)

Kimberli also co-writes the Charity Styles Caribbean Thriller series with Best-selling author, Wayne Stinnett.

She loves sharing her passion for adventure and wildlife with her readers and happily gives away some of her award-winning wildlife photos. Sign up for her newsletter at www.kimberlibindschatel.com and get a free photograph for your desktop.

Join the adventure.

What will Poppy do next?

OPERATION
WOLF
PACK

Book SEVEN
a Poppy McVie
Adventure

KIMBERLI A. BINDSCHATEL

A bloodthirsty monster stalks the Idaho mountains.
Terrified locals are desperate for help.
One woman is ready to take out the real culprit.

Feisty Special Agent Poppy McVie is on a case in the west—stop
the beast that's hunting the livestock under the cover of night. The
ranchers are convinced nearby wolf packs are to blame and are
ready to shoot the animals on sight. Poppy demands they stop, but
she's shoved aside.

　Desperate for clues to the real perp, she kicks the investigation
into high gear. What she finds is far more terrifying than she ever
imagined. Can she expose the truth in time, or will the next victim
be her?

50726252R00137

Made in the USA
Middletown, DE
27 June 2019